TO DREAM ......

Ralph Mancini, an officer in the United Nations Law Enforcement Agency, is dedicated to the world-wide War on Drugs. A new drug is developed, giving a uniquely effective 'trip', whereby people become God-like beings and they experience 'heaven'. The next trip is their only priority — whatever the cost. Ralph and Inspector Frere follow a tangled trail of murder, seeking the source of the peril — but will they be too late to stop it spreading across the world?

E. C . TUBB

TO DREAM AGAIN

Complete and Unabridged

LINFORD
Leicester

First published in Great Britain

First Linford Edition
published 2011

British Library CIP Data

Tubb, E. C.
    To dream again. - - (Linford mystery library)
    1. United Nations Office on Drugs and Crime
    - -Officials and employees- -Fiction.
    2. Hallucinogenic drugs- -Fiction. 3. Drug
    control- -Fiction. 4. Suspense fiction.
    5. Large type books.
    I. Title II. Series
    823.9'14–dc22

    ISBN 978–1–4448–0774–5

1.

Ralph Mancini smelt the odour of carnations and recognised Cybele's distinctive perfume. She'd come through the shadowed darkness to stand quietly at his side, head tilted so that the soft light from the sky shone on the smooth contours of her face, the dark wells of her eyes. Standing there she resembled an ancient Grecian statue. An anachronism here on this penthouse garden a mile above the streets of the city. Then she moved a little and the spell was broken.

'It's beautiful,' she said. 'Beautiful!'

Together they looked up and over the parapet to where the broad arc of Halley's comet hung like a glowing scimitar in the sky.

'Beautiful,' she said again, and added, 'No wonder the sight of it used to upset the old-timers.'

'They though it a visitation from the gods,' he said quietly. 'A terrible omen of dreadful things to come.'

'Superstition.'

'Perhaps. But when it appeared in 1910 the world, as people then knew it, shortly ceased to exist. The First World War,' he explained. 'That wrecked the social order and redrew national boundaries which laid the basis for World War Two. And you know what happened after that.'

'Atomic power,' she said. 'Intercontinental transportation. Space travel. Computers . . . I see what you mean. But those were good things, not bad. They led to progress. And after the comet came again in 1985 we've had the internet, genetic engineering and countless medical advances.'

'And this time?'

'Nothing. You're no mystic. You don't believe in omens and all that rubbish. No one does in this day and age.'

Her tone was dogmatic, brooking no argument, but he had no intention of arguing despite his annoyance that she had sought him out and broken his introspection. Cybele Howarth was his hostess and it was both impolite and impolitic to be rude.

'It's beautiful anyway,' he said. 'And rare. You'll be almost a hundred years old before you get the chance to see it again.'

It was a diplomatic lie but she didn't correct him as to her true age. Instead she said, 'No, it'll hang around for a while yet.'

'You're being precise, Cybele. When it goes it will be seventy-five years before it returns. That's a long time.'

Long enough for the entire world to change. He looked again at the comet wondering how many who saw it now would be alive to see it then. Not many, he guessed, only the very young and the very rich if they were not too old. Not over thirty, say, which put him five years on the wrong side even if he had the money to buy extended life, which he hadn't.

He was seeing Halley's Comet for the first and last time.

It was a sobering thought and he concentrated on the spectacle oblivious to the pulsing beat of music rising from the floor below. Any excuse was good enough for the Party crowd to throw a party and

Cybele had really let herself go. An astronomical affair with everyone in appropriate costume. But of all the guests only he and she and a handful of others had bothered to step into the garden to look at the comet.

'Ralph.' Beside him the woman moved, restless, impatient. 'Come on, now. You've looked at that thing long enough. I didn't invite you here just to stargaze. Anyway,' she added. 'I'm having it filmed so you'll be able to see it again if you want to.'

An invitation? Anything was possible and his job held certain glamour for the uninitiated. Or was it perhaps more than that? His eyes searched her face, falsely young in the subdued illumination, but saw nothing other than a mask of superbly applied cosmetics. He looked at her eyes, glowing with reflected comet-light, the pupils apparently normal. He looked away before his scrutiny became obvious.

'Well?' Her voice held amusement. 'Did you like what you looked at?'

Deliberately he was obtuse. 'The comet? It is almost the loveliest thing I've ever seen.'

'Almost?'

'You, Cybele, outshine everything in the sky. Alone I could appreciate the comet. With you at my side its glory seems less.'

'Flattery?'

'The truth.'

Her hand closed on his bare arm, tightened. 'It was kind of you to say that, Ralph, but you disappoint me. A policeman should never try to act the gallant. He should be hard, tough, ruthless. That's what I find so attractive about you — you look that way. 'Don't spoil the image with soft words.'

'I apologise.'

'Now you're making things worse.'

'Then go to Hell!'

'That's better.' Her smile was radiant. 'Shall we go there together?'

Hell rested at the foot of thirty curving steps of transparent crystal, an artistic depiction of Pluto, a red-lit place of noise and smoke and confusion. Blue, green and silver draped the walls, the chilliness of the colours counterbalanced with swathes of red and gold. Bubbles drifted lamely in the air, popped they gusted sweet perfumes or nauseous vapours. Strobe lights flashed in hypnotic tempo and a ten-piece group blasted amplified sound.

'Hi, tall, dark and handsome!' A girl swayed from between the drifting balloons. She was naked aside from bands of body-paint around hips and breasts and carried a tray of drinks. One of the dozen waitresses hired for the occasion, sparkling, eager to please. 'Help yourself.'

She watched as he took a glass.

'I'm Saturn,' she said abruptly. 'See my rings? And you're Mars. Man! You've got muscle! If you're ma's then I'd sure like to see pa's.' She giggled, amused at her humour. 'Have another drink.'

'Not yet,' said Ralph.

'Come on!' she urged. 'Get loaded! When you're ready to shoot just come looking.'

She moved away, tray held high, buttocks undulating an invitation. A big-breasted Rhea slapped them as the girl passed. A Juno ran a hand caressingly over her flank. An Eros, wearing only paint and a laurel wreath, smiled as he helped himself to a drink.

'She's young,' said Cybele condescendingly. 'Riding high and enjoying every minute. You fancy her?'

'No.'

'Why not? She's young, pretty and you made a big impression.'

'And is that reason enough for me to want her?'

'Well, isn't it?'

Ralph shook his head. 'I stopped being a reactive mechanism ten years ago. After the first five hundred they're all the same. Now I need something else,' he said. 'A personality. And I want to be wanted for me as an individual and not just because I happen to be around.'

Cybele laughed. 'You're showing your age, Ralph. That's the way women used to talk years ago. Maybe you should take a little something to restore your interest in life.'

'Life spelt S.E.X.?'

'You're cynical,' she said. 'That's what comes of being a policeman. Now drink up and join the party.'

The glass held a combination of rum and brandy both at least twelve years old. He sipped, tasting the blend, recognising nothing other than normal alcohols. Not that Cybele would have been stupid enough to add illegal ingredients but sometimes the caterers got ambitious or a guest might have spiked the drinks. And there was always the possibility of sabotage.

He sipped again, irritated with himself for his preoccupation, his eternal suspicions. It was, as the woman had pointed out, the result of his job. To be forever watchful, always on duty, always looking for the worst. Well, to hell with it! Tonight he would have fun.

The group fell silent, recommencing with a peculiar melody of flutes and pipes, the wail of strings and the hypnotic tap of a drum. A dozen Balinese dancers swirled on the floor, light winking from their elaborate costumes as they went through the mechanical perfection of a native dance. Against the near-nudity of the guests they looked bizarre, robot-like in their posturing, fantastically over-dressed and yet, oddly enough, the more erotic because of it.

The lure of mystery, thought Ralph watching. The desire to see what lay beneath the shielding garments. The age-old attraction of the half-concealed against the wholly revealed. In the Western world flesh had become a debased currency.

He turned away as the dance ended, feeling detached, bored with the empty gaiety. A girl ran up to him, laughing, stabbing at a drifting balloon. He held his breath against the stink of asafoetida, caught a naked arm, crushed another of the bubbles against her smiling face. The clean tang of pine filled the air.

'You lost!' shrieked the girl. 'Now pay a forfeit!'

'Later.'

'Now!' she demanded. 'Hey, Max!' She waved across the room. 'This guy lost and now he won't pay.'

'He pick a sweet one?' Max, like Ralph, was wearing the classical costume of a Roman Legionnaire. It displayed his gymnasium-trained figure to its best advantage. He smiled with a flash of white teeth but his eyes held violence. 'Come on, sport. You bet and you lost. Now the little lady calls the tune. What'll it be, honey?'

'Grip him,' she said. 'Bring him to his knees.'

'And kiss your feet? O.K.' Max held out his hand. 'Come on, sport. Let's shake.'

Ralph drained his glass and passed it to a willing hand. The strobe lights were beginning to get him, firing his blood with incipient hysteria, adding to the relentless pounding of the music with its jungle-rhythm appeal to the primitive.

Thoughtfully he looked at the other man. Max stood before him, legs straddled, right hand extended. He still smiled but his eyes held cruelty. He would take his opponent's hand and squeeze it, forcing him to his knees, whimpering from the pain of crushed bones. A touch of sadism beneath a mask of civilised fun. A chance to see a fellow man grovel and so enhance his own concept of masculinity

'Come on, sport,' he said again. 'Don't keep the lady waiting. Ralph took the proffered hand, conscious of the circle in which they stood, the rapt and staring eyes. Together they tightened their grip.

There were ways to dodge it, Ralph knew. He could have thrust his own hand well forward so that the webs between thumbs and forefingers met and so negated the pressure. The hand within his own was short of skin but padded with muscle, strong, trained in gymnastic exercise, but where Max had trained for fun Ralph had trained for real. He summoned strength from his back and shoulders, biceps and forearm, and fed it into his hand. He felt muscles yield, the shift of bone.

'Down,' he said quietly. 'On your knees.'

Max sucked in his breath. He was no longer smiling and the cruelty in his eyes had been replaced by hate. Sweat glistened on his forehead and ran in tiny rivulets down his face. For a long moment they stood, straining, then he made a small sound deep in his throat and, abruptly, was down on his knees.

'My feet,' said Ralph, maintaining the

11

pressure, and then changed his mind. It was wrong to press a man too far. 'No. The girl's feet. Kiss them.'

She laughed at the touch of the lips, a silly, inane giggle. 'Why, Max! I didn't know you cared!'

He glowered as he rose to the sound of laughter. His hand was white streaked with red and the nails were rimmed with seeping blood. 'You bastard' he said looking at Ralph. 'I'll get you for this!'

'Any time, Max. Now if you like.'

'Later will do. You — '

'That will do, Max!' Cybele stepped between them, cool, imperious. 'I've warned you before about your party games. You play too rough but this time you picked on the wrong man. He won and that's all there is to it. Now let's all have a drink to celebrate his victory.' She slipped her arm through Ralph's and led him aside as the circle dissolved. 'Feeling better?'

'Should I be?'

'Of course. You're a man and men are supposed to enjoy violence.' Her face became momentarily bleak. 'Too much

12

sometimes, especially when they can take it out on a woman. Any girl who goes with Max tonight will be asking for all she gets.'

'We were talking about men,' said Ralph quietly. 'Not the things that call themselves that and have to keep on proving it.' He glanced to where his recent opponent stood among his syco-phants gulping a drink. 'If I stepped out of line there I apologise. Would you like me to leave?'

Her fingers rested warm on his naked arm. 'Don't be a fool Ralph. If I wanted you to go you wouldn't have to ask. Forget him. I'll have a talk with Max later and tell him what he obviously doesn't know. Now there are some people I think you'd like to meet.'

2

They sat in a small room with padded walls, the heavy door a barricade against the noise. The furnishings were old-fashioned, deep armchairs of polished leather, tables of real wood, the carpet of deep-piled wool. Bottles and glasses were in evidence and the air was heavy with the smoke of burning tobacco. One wall was almost entirely covered by a flat television screen, which showed a montage of riots. One of the men switched it off and Cybele made the introductions.

'Professor Thesiger, emeritus of Harvard. Conrad Lanchester, curator of the Smithsonian Museum. Andrew Dwyer, writer. John Rigby, drama critic.' She turned to Ralph. 'And this is Major Ralph Mancini of the United Nations Law Enforcement Agency. If you want a good argument he is your man. But don't challenge him. He almost crushed Max Brannon's hand to a pulp.'

'Serve the young pup right!' Professor Thesiger was a big, round man of about seventy. He wore a rumpled toga stained with cigar ash and his broad face was mottled with the signs of good living. He squinted up at Ralph. 'A policeman, eh? Caught any murderers lately?'

'That isn't my job,' said Ralph easily. 'We don't interfere in local jurisdiction.'

He sat down as Cybele leaned over him towards the table, the scent of her perfume sharp against the odours of tobacco and liquor. 'A drink, Ralph? Brandy?'

'Thank you.'

She handed him a glass and straightened. 'Well, I'll leave you boys to chat a while. Have fun.'

Thesiger gusted his breath as she left the room, the closing door cutting off the jumble of sounds from the party-room outside. 'A fine woman, Cybele. A damn fine woman. Did you ever meet her husband?'

'No,' said Ralph. 'But isn't he dead?'

'Three years ago,' said Lanchester. He was about sixty, bald, dressed like the professor in a toga. Two Jupiters holding court. 'He was nasty swine with a penchant for using a whip in bed. God knows how Cybele stood it as long as she did but I suppose she must have been in love with him at one time. The way he died was poetic justice.'

Ralph sipped at his brandy. 'How did he die?'

Dwyer was a thin-faced, intense-looking man of about forty wearing a winged and pleated garo. A Mercury with a chip on his shoulder. Sourly, he said: 'They found him in a hotel room and the verdict was death caused by over-stimulation of the vagus. That part was made public knowledge. What they didn't publish was the fact that he'd been playing games with some well-built girl and she's sat on him too hard and for too long.'

'Suffocated,' said Rigby thoughtfully. He was the same age as Dwyer and had come as Neptune. 'I wrote a play based on that theme once but they wouldn't touch it. Not because of the sex angle but because too many people might get the wrong idea.' Rigby helped himself to more whisky. 'Conrad?'

'Just a little.' Lanchester leaned back and drew thoughtfully at his antique pipe. 'An UNLEA man,' he said to Ralph. 'In my book that means only one thing. Narcotics. Am I right?'

'Not quite. We do other things.'

'Such as hunting down political assassins and keeping a watch on arms shipments,' agreed Lanchester. 'But your real job is the suspension of drugs. It has to be. A worldwide racket needs a worldwide police force to combat it. But how do you operate? You can't have that many personnel.'

'We don't need them,' explained Ralph, and wondered why he should need to explain at all. Surely these men would know how the United Nations operated? 'I've high rank because that gives me superiority and with it I can demand the full cooperation of any local force. National forces too if I need to use them. All it requires is a little diplomacy but most people are helpful and every officer wants to crush the racket.'

'Racket?' Dwyer raised his eyebrows. 'If the desire to supply a demand is a racket then every business in the world falls into that category.'

'Now you're playing with words,' snorted Thesiger. 'That's the trouble with you writers, you're always playing with words. You know damn well what a racket is, what supply and demand is and what legitimate business is. If we're going to have a discussion for God's sake keep it rational.'

'All right,' said Dwyer. 'Let's see if you're willing to abide by your own rules.' Leaning forward he rapped a fingernail against one of the bottles. 'Whisky. Addictive, destructive, expensive in both man-hours of production and the misuse of grain. But legal and therefore permitted. Why?'

Thesiger was curt. 'There is a demand for whisky and a drink never hurt a man yet.'

'Maybe one day you'll ask the relative of a dipsomaniac to verify that,' said Dwyer quietly. 'But let's take your other contention. There is a demand for whisky.

True. But is it a natural demand? If so why do the distilling companies spend billions on advertising? They don't do it to push their own particular product because mergers have made that a farce. They do it simply to create a demand. Alcohol is a drug. If the open sale of one drug is legal when why not another?'

Lanchester knocked ash from his pipe. 'There is a high tax on liquor. No government can afford to lose the revenue.'

'So, in the U.S. alone, ten million people are chronic drunkards and they are only the ones we know about. But that's all right because the government collects from their misery.' Dwyer lit a cigarette. 'All right, forget that, I'm not moralising on the evils of alcohol. But if it's a question of revenue then why not tax the soft drugs? And before any of you get on your high horse I'll ask our lawman here one question. Is there any medical proof whatsoever that marijuana is more harmful than tobacco?'

Ralph sipped at his brandy. He had been in such arguments before and he wondered why he should be in one now.

The coincidence of his job and the subject under discussion was a little too raw. Quietly he said. 'Leave me out of this. I don't make the laws I just carry them out.'

'You've answered by default,' said Dwyer triumphantly. 'There isn't and you know it. So why ban it and the other innocuous compounds medical science has discovered and which can alleviate our misery?'

'By 'ban', of course, you mean why aren't they on open sale.' Rigby pursed his lips. 'Every user of hard drugs has graduated from the soft ones. Let everyone have access to them and you'll wind up with a nation of addicts.'

'That's crap and you know it!' Dwyer was getting a little hot under the collar. Or he was pretending to be? 'Every mainliner has drunk milk. By your logic the drinking of milk leads directly to the use of hard drugs. Therefore, ban milk. If we're going to argue for God's sake forget misleading propaganda and deal in facts. Fact one is that there is no medical proof that the soft drugs are physically harmful.'

'That isn't quite right.' Lanchester

spoke from behind a cloud of smoke. 'There must have been articles written on the subject.'

'That isn't proof. That's guff churned out for popular consumption to create an artificial bogeyman. Dire speculation and the use of misleading verbiage designed to scare the ignorant. And it's no accident that it's all one-sided. We all know that the government controls the means of mass communication and if you're going to tell me that we have no censorship then I can assure you we have. Damn it, these days even the internet is regulated by Government censors. I know!'

'You're getting excited,' said Thesiger. 'At least paedophiles can no longer peddle child pornography on the net as they used to do. Have another drink and simmer down.'

'Head in the sand, Professor? Is that what you taught at Harvard? If you see something you don't like, close your eyes and make believe that it doesn't exist?'

'Calm down, Andrew, and get off your soapbox,' said Rigby. 'Let's find out what's happening to the world.'

He rose and, finding a remote, switched on the television. Sound and colour filled the room as he resumed his chair and Ralph wondered if he was being diplomatic or if this too was calculated. Annoyed with himself he took more brandy. Again he was being over-suspicious and reading hidden motives into every innocent occurrence. Even intellectuals needed recreation and the subjects of conversation had been normal enough. And yet he had the feeling that he was being manoeuvred and he didn't like it.

Sipping his brandy he stared at the screen.

It was much the same as before. A montage of views gathered by satellite cameras from the major cities of the world and all harping on the same theme. Riots, protests, demonstrations. Armoured police using nerve gas, water cannon, clubs and guns to disperse milling crowds of civilians. Some places were worse than others. In Delhi they used machine guns, in Peking napalm. Europe was blander and favoured the use of vomiting agents. Closer to home riot guns flung showers of anaesthetising agents. A feast of vicarious violence to titivate the viewer.

It was the comet, of course. Religious factions saw it as a sign that the Second Coming was at hand. Others as a sign for them to rise against their real or imagined oppressors. Still more used it as an excuse to go on a rampage and grab a little fun.

Finishing his brandy Ralph set down the glass, rose and left the room.

Outside the party had died a little with bodies sprawled in open abandon. A titan caressed a Juno. Two Saturns blended their body-paint beneath the weight of a Rhea. Eron and Impetus shared Dione. Venus lived up to her name. Looking for the toilets Ralph opened a door and found himself in a bedroom. The couch was fully occupied. Slumped on the floor a dozen youngsters ringed a comer bowl suspended over a burning lamp. They watched, dull-eyed, as he investigated the mixture it contained. Hot water, menthol and carbon tetrachloride. The vapour would be interesting even if the excitement it created was mostly the product of imagination. But they had tried.

They always tried.

In the toilet he washed, regretting having drunk the last brandy, hating the loss of the fine edge of concentration. Bleakly he stared into the mirror wondering just why he had come. He didn't like parties with their meaningless drinking and noise. He didn't like the people who came to them with their shallow interests and pretended concern. So why had he bothered? He knew that answer and didn't like it. The Pent Crowd was important and invitations too often refused ceased to be extended. And Cybele had been insistent.

Thought of his hostess made him hesitate as he left the toilet. It would be impolite to leave without wishing her farewell and thanking her for the party yet he couldn't see her in the main room. He thrust his way through the few remaining bubbles and seemingly catatonic dancers checking every Venus in sight who was unoccupied but not finding Cybele. She could be up on the roof, of course, and it was a good reason for him to climb the stairs and take another look at the comet.

Then, if he still couldn't find her, he would leave.

Outside it was cool with a soft breeze rustling the fronds of the flowering plants. They were always flowering, changed when the blooms began to wilt, replaced by others still in bud. He walked across the turf towards the parapet and stood looking at the city.

It was quiet tonight.

Quiet or not he couldn't hear it, the sharp edge of his mind dulled by alcohol, but he didn't think it was wholly that. The traffic sent up its usual susurration and the glow from countless lights dulled the stars but the pulse of the city was slow and turgid as if the beast had been numbed by the splendour of the heavens. He looked at it, the great tail low now and almost touching the summit of the red-lit cylinder that was Dexter Prison, the topmost lights of which glowed fifteen hundred feet above the ground.

Gravel crunched and he turned, stepping away from the parapet, thinking of Max and his threats of revenge. Then he caught the scent of a distinctive perfume and saw the woman standing in the shadowed darkness, still and as beautiful as a Grecian statue.

'Cybele! I've been looking for you.'

'I knew you'd come up for a last look at the comet, Ralph. I've been waiting for you.'

A lover's tryst? He doubted it and as she approached and he could see the strain on her face matching the tension in her voice he was sure of it. Sure too that his suspicions had not been unfounded.

'I've got to leave,' he said quickly. 'It's been a wonderful party and thank you for having invited me.'

'Ralph!' Her hand caught his arm as he turned to move away. 'Don't go. Not yet.'

'Please!' He drew a deep breath. 'I know what you're going to say, Cybele, but please don't. I don't want to hear it. Just let me leave as I intended.'

'No!' Her hand tightened on his arm. 'You like me, Ralph. I know that. And you work for UNLEA and would have access. It's such a small thing really. All I want is a little — please, Ralph. You won't regret it.'

He looked down at her, the comet-light reflected from her eyes, wild now, desperate. It was no satisfaction to know that he had been right all along, that his trained instinct had not let him down. The whole thing had been designed to lead him to this moment. The invitation, her insistence that he accept, the proximity and display of wealth, even the intellectuals to whom he had been introduced and the topics of conversation chosen so as to soften him up. To condition him to agree.

The one thing he could never do.

'Tell me something, Cybele. Have you taken it already?'

Her silence was his answer.

'You poor bitch,' he said softly. 'God, I feel sorry for you. You poor, hopeless, stupid bitch!'

In the light of the comet her tears shone like pearls but it was too late for regret.

3

Edward Dexter was dead, but his evil lived after him in the shape of the prison that bore his name. He had designed and built a monstrous phallic symbol to threaten the sky. A vast tube of windowless concrete, ugly, bleak. Inside a hundred floors each held a hundred cells and each cell held three prisoners. They had tiered bunks, a table, chairs, toilet and washing facilities. They had a view through bars and a repeater television screen to remind them of the world outside. They wore paper clothing and ate processed pap and every day thirty thousand men cursed the Dexter name

Curses, like prayers, have a tangibility of their own. Raw anger was nothing, it was expected and preferred. It was the sullen hate that followed it, the helpless rage of men who feel their individuality slipping away that was the trouble. It contaminated the entire building and affected all the staff from the warden down to the lowliest guard. The radiated, futile protest of men who were forced to think and act as if they were unproductive battery hens. Waking, eating, watching, eating, sleeping if and when they could. Some men slept a lot. Others hardly at all. They were the dangerous ones.

Dangerous but only to themselves or their cellmates. Which was why they wore paper clothing so mechanically weak it could never be used to fashion a rope. And why, among other reasons, there were always three men to a cell.

In number 875 Lassogone knew that he was going mad.

He lay supine on his bunk, staring at the concrete two feet above his face, bread wadded in his ears to gain the privacy of silence. Always he thought of the same thing, which is why he knew he was going insane. For the thing possessing him was the obsession to escape. And there could be no escape. Consciously he knew it but still his mind examined the concept, sniffed at it, circled around it, gnawed at it like a rat worrying cheese.

The toilet, for example. The sewage had to go somewhere and that somewhere was down. If he could manage to break into the channel it might be possible to descend to the ground level, to the main sewers, perhaps to crawl or float along them until they vented themselves into the procession plant. A man wasn't sewage. He would be able to dodge the filters and chemicals and get clear. Then to find a worker and take his clothing. To walk out and away.

Free!

But this cell was a high number and on a high floor. Maybe the channel wouldn't be wide enough so high. If he could get to a lower cell then there would be more room to accommodate the accumulated waste. But how to get to a lower floor and how to break into the channel if he could?

Around and around. Nibble, nibble.

Try another way. Through the bars, say. If he was sick the medics would come for him. He could play around and pretend to be unconscious. Then, when they were off guard, he could rise up and tackle the officers. Kill them if he had to. Then to

30

change clothes and pretend to be on the staff. He could use the elevator to descend and watch for a chance to leave. Hide in a truck, maybe. Who would question a man in uniform? He could get a ride into the city and grab some civilian clothes and money. He'd be out and away.

Free!

But when the medics came they always shot a prisoner full of Pentothal. And the elevator would be guarded. And he wouldn't have the strength to overcome the officers and even if he had he wasn't sure of the procedure downstairs. They would have a system of checking and he would be caught before he had a chance.

Nibble, nibble. Around and around.

How about asking for an interview with the warden? He could fake some excuse, wanting to confess to a previous crime, maybe. Then, when he was upstairs with the Big Guy, he would grab his throat and threaten to kill him unless they let him go. Then . . .

The razor-sharp teeth of madness gnawing at his brain.

Kelman wasn't going insane he was just

getting mad. He closed his big hands as he glared at the television screen feeling his temper beginning to boil. Some nerd was skelling a set of dissonancy chimes with a dozen loblolly girls gyrating in the background; the whole thing served up in day glow with a two-second subliminal flicker which had he been able to read it, said RE CONNECT.

Bastedo wasn't as sensitive. He sat grinning as the kid finished his act, fingernails rasping the electro-sensitive surface of the chimes as the dozen near-nudes rotated breasts and buttocks in tantalising abandon.

'Nice show, uh?'

Kelman glowered. He was no masochist and the sight of the girls had upset him. His sexual appetite was normal and the alternatives available were unsatisfying. Curtly he said. 'It's a load of crap.'

'You've no artistic appreciation,' said Bastedo still enjoying the show. 'That kid pulls down more in a month than you've handled in your entire life. That means he's smart. A hell of a lot smarter than you are.'

'So he's rich. Does that make him good?'

'He's good.' Against the bulk of the other man Bastedo was small, his face sharp with the shrewd eyes of a rodent. His teeth were small, pointed, gleaming as he spoke. 'Better than you. He's walking around and what are you doing? You're waiting, that's what. Waiting until your stretch is up and you can walk out of this dump. And then what?'

'Then maybe I won't have to look and listen to a bunch of nerds all day and half the night.' Kelman glared at the screen. 'Look at him! Look at those girls!'

'You're envious.' Bastedo turned from the screen and leaned back in his chair. He was smiling but his eyes held a cold calculation. 'That kid makes you look what you are. A failure. A so-called tough guy who said 'boo' and who wound up doing three years in the pen. That character's out there with a nice collection of female comfort and you call him dumb. Man! Do you need educating!'

'Stuff it.' Kelman was defensive, uneasily conscious of the truth in what the other said. 'He's just lucky. I know a hundred guys who could do what he does and do it a damn sight better.'

'Then why aren't they doing it?'

'I told you. They didn't get the breaks. It's just a matter of luck.'

'Listen,' said Bastedo emphatically. 'You've got it all wrong. That kid's not lucky, he's smart. He went out of his way to meet the right people. He crawled, ate dirt, laughed at crummy jokes. He used everything that came his way in order to climb to the top and he's made it. Luck? Hell, man, only a failure needs luck. That boy's got brains.'

Kelman snorted but he felt deflated. Luck or not the kid had two things he wanted. Freedom and cash. The nerd could go where he liked and do as he pleased. He could get drunk, go to the private fights, buy any dame on the market, do things in real style. Why? Because, as Bastedo had said, he had the brains to reach out and get what he wanted. And himself?

Three years for trying to rob a store.

As usual he'd made the play single-handed figuring that what no one knew they couldn't spill. They couldn't spill. They couldn't put the finger on him and sell him short for the reward. It was a good system and had kept him running free for ten years but this time he'd miscalculated. The store wasn't empty as he'd thought. A nerd of an under-manager had stayed behind with his secretary to 'check stock' and they saw him as they emerged. One he could have taken care of but not both so he'd yielded figuring it would help his plea.

His lawyer had sighed. 'Mercy? What the hell are you talking about? You want the court to be gentle because you didn't kill anyone when you had the chance? You want paying for not having commit-ted murder? Listen, idiot, you forget that line of argument. You were broke, desper-ate to buy medical attention for your sick mother. You were tempted and fell. A hell of a defence but what else have we?'

Nothing. So he drew three years in the Dexter jail and no one seemed to worry about his fictitious mother which was a hell of a thing had she been real and he her only support as claimed.

It was a long time to spend in coop.

He rose and walked five steps down the length of the cell and leaned on the bars. Outside lay the central column containing the elevator, the guard, the communications network. The baths where once a week he took a shower. The room where once a month his hair was cropped short. They were the only times he left his cell.

Behind him, corpse-like, Lassogone toyed with another segment of his obsession.

He could get religious and ask to see a minister. Play the game all along the line so that he was trusted and maybe allowed to go to church. Hell, there had to be a church. Then, when the guy was off-guard, he'd grab him and take his clothes. By that time he'd know the procedure and would be able to head for the way out. He could bust himself in the nose and shield his face, tell anyone who asked that he'd fallen. They wouldn't question a man of God. He could walk out into the street and leave Dexter behind.

Free!

But prisoners weren't supposed to be

religious and, if they were, that was just too damn bad. They'd get a bible and a heap of tracts and twice a day services were held on the television screens. There was no minister, not even visiting social workers, no one who would listen to him.

The rat that was his thoughts moved around to gnaw elsewhere.

Maybe he should go crazy. Scream and yell and act up like he'd lost his marbles. The medics would come and shoot him full of dope, knocking him out for safe and easy transport to the hospital. There, maybe, he could wait his chance. Lie low until the night shift came on and the attendants were careless. Until the lights were low and he could slip out of bed and grab himself a uniform and head for the big outside.

Free!

But there was no night shift and the lights were never turned low and the medics took no chances. He'd wind up doped, shocked, his brains seared with jolting current. He'd be strapped down or put in a cell and the only difference would be that the cell would be smaller

37

and padded and he'd never leave it because no psycho was ever discharged from jail. Never.

Dear God! Dear sweet, God! He mustn't go mad!

Kelman turned from the bars, walked five paces, turned, took three more and slumped at the table. The picture on the screen had changed. Now it showed snow-covered slopes and brightly dressed skiers, soaring pines and a sun that threw a golden light. Ideal entertainment for men who lived in concrete boxes and had no natural light, no natural air.

The holiday-scene was faded out to show a championship football match played under floodlights, which faded out to show a soap opera, which faded out to give a view of the comet with an unctuous voice relating its history. Three minutes were enough and the view of the sky was replaced by that of a phoney nightclub with girls, songs and dancing. Impossible smiles from impossible people in an impossible world.

Bastedo sucked in his breath. 'You know, Jack' he said to Kelman. 'There's a hell of a lot waiting out there if you've got the guts to reach for it.'

Loblolly girls with overdeveloped breasts and buttocks — tall, slim girls with boyish figures — round, plump women with the fiery passion of the south — ice-cold drinks — the resort at Polar North — real meat with shape and flavour — beds ten feet square with pneumatic cushions — liquor — travel — girls — girls — girls.

The subliminal flicker on the television screen said; YOU ARE TIRED.

Kelman yawned. 'Sure,' he said sarcastically. 'A hell of a lot. I collected three years. You got six months. I guess we could both get life if we put our minds to it.'

'So what's to lose?' Bastedo glanced up to where the nub of the spy-mike watched with its electronic eye and ear. Maybe the guard was concentrating on this cell, maybe not; it was a hundred to one against but why take a chance? He leaned over the table, hands busy with a worn deck of cards. 'Listen,' he said quietly as he dealt. 'Pick up the cards and make as if you're playing.'

Kelman frowned at his hand, lips barely moving. 'You want to talk?'

'I've been watching you. You're not like that other nerd.' Bastedo didn't glance to where Lassogone examined the destruction of his mind. 'He's gone. Crazy. We'll have to watch him all the time. But you've managed to beat the game. That takes strength and guts — two things I can use. Interested?'

'I like working alone.'

Bastedo played a card and picked up the trick. 'A good idea but sometimes it pays to have a little help. Two can be better than one.'

'That depends on who they are. You're in here. That makes you a loser. I've had enough bad luck of my own.'

'The hell with it!' said Bastedo loudly. He scooped up the cards and began to deal. 'Let's play for something real. The loser stays awake to watch our friend.' Quietly he said, 'I was picked up in a street-search and was carrying a cane. Six months for having an offensive weapon and they didn't want to know about my bum ankle. A couple of strikes against you and you haven't got a chance. You'll find out.'

'So?'

'So get smart, make a pile and quit.' The pasteboards made little rustling noises as they fell to the table. 'I'm getting out in two days time. You get sprung a bit later. If you itch for the big time look me up. If you're scared then forget it.'

'What's on your mind?' Kelman played an ace, picked up the trick. 'You got a scheme?'

'Nuts to that. In here we don't talk. Just forget the whole thing. But when you get out look me up. Mother Hastings on Fifty-three and Luna. You ask for me and wait around if you have to. It could be that I've got just what you're needing.'

He swore as Kelman won the game. 'Damn the luck!'

'O.K.,' said Kelman, and didn't smile until he was in the old, familiar position with his back to the spy-mike and his face to the wall.

4

It was a good match with the odds going at five to one against the challenger drawing within thirty; two to one against him snatching the crown. He was better than anticipated. Twenty-six seconds after the gong his blade stroked blood from the defender's ribs. A hundred and fifteen later he stood victorious over a lacerated heap.

He hadn't killed but the one-time champion would never fight again. Surgery could repair the slashed muscle and sinew but his nerve had broken. It would have been more merciful to have punctured his heart.

Frank Atwater scowled and tore his betting slip to shreds. Around him, tight-packed in the private stadium, other disgruntled punters added to the thrown confetti. They were few because, of necessity, the stadium had to be small but even so their massed body-heat had caused the temperature to climb into the nineties. Frank mopped his face as the gong called for silence.

'Ladies and Gentlemen!' The M.C. was impeccably dressed and unfairly cool as he stood in the twenty-foot ring. 'For your pleasure the next bout will be a melee between two men and two girls. Clubs will be used and the winners will extract the normal penalty.'

It was a predictable item. The men would win and take from the girls what they wanted. What every man in the place wanted and would vicariously enjoy. The women too. They would shriek with simulated outrage at the public rape but they would enjoy it all the same. Enjoy it even more should the men lose.

Voyeurs, thought Atwater looking around the stadium at the painted and raddled cheeks, the sagging jowls and balding heads. We're all nothing but a bunch of damn voyeurs. We watch others fight and bleed because we're too scared to risk our own skins. We watch others fornicate because we're jaded and can't —

He checked himself. Can't what? Get

sexual fulfilment by personal activity? Do the things we reckon we should be capable of doing? Face our own inadequacy?

Impotence, he thought dully. A spreading disease. Born of satiation and from unlimited sexual congress when young. And now that we've reached the fifties what have we left? Sex is an old, tired story and how many variations can there be on a single theme? Adventure is out. Fighting is dangerous. Gambling gets to be a bore. Drinking gets monotonous. So we watch and envy and kid ourselves that we're having a hell of a time.

A hell of a time.

He liked the phrase and repeated it, savouring the words and their inner meaning. It summed up the time so well. Too many people, too little room. Too much accent on the quest for pleasure and too little room. Too little opportunity for real freedom of choice. In this age liberty was a sound without meaning.

The gong clashed. Four nude bodies entered the ring and the watchers sucked in their breath in delight and anticipation.

The management had been clever. The men were old, over fifty, grotesque with sagging flesh and swollen paunches. The girls were in their teens, firm, lithe and agile. Clubs made exciting sounds as they smacked against yielding flesh.

The gong again. Two men dressed in gleaming armour, perfect facsimiles of the knights of romantic legend. They carried maces shields, swords slung over their shoulders, daggers hanging at their belts. One was in shining silver the other in gleaming gold. The armour was thin, easily crushed and of little real defence. The men inside were meat ready-canned for quick disposal.

'Even money on either,' announced the speakers. 'Two to one against silver getting beaten with a mace. Three to one against gold falling to the sword.'

Atwater frowned at the betting machine on the back of the seat before him. He fed a card into the slot and thumbed buttons to make his choice, a slip of paper spitting into his hand. If he won he could cash it at the same machine.

The crowd hushed as the fighters

settled down to business. Novelty items were always of interest and this pair were good. Gold used a fast underarm swing that sent the spiked head of his mace slamming against the lower edge of his opponent's shield. Silver countered by retreating and lashing sidewise. Gold caught the blow on his shield and moved forward pressing silver back against the ropes. For a while they exchanged blows and then gold saw his chance. His mace swept upwards, hitting the lower edge of silver's shield and knocking it high. Gold moved in, fast, the mace cutting air. It slammed against the unprotected side. The spikes dug into the armour and held. The crowd rose, shrieking, as silver smashed his own mace down on the golden helmet.

Blood sprayed from the buckled visor. Again silver plied his mace, a third time. The helmet shattered like an egg. Gold staggered, lifted his hands as if to protect himself, then crashed to the floor.

Atwater relaxed. It was nice to win and nicer still to sit warm and well fed and comfortable while others suffered for his pleasure. But they had always suffered. Years ago in the select houses with the understanding madams and the willing girls. The whips and manacles and rubber sheets. The exhibitions and films of torture and pain. Someone was always around to supply a demand.

He lit a cigar, turning as someone squeezed into the seat at his side. 'Ned! What the hell are you doing here?'

'I'm a member. Didn't you know?'

Atwater frowned. Ned Lacey was short, round and inclined to sweat. His lips were a little too full, his hips a little too broad and his reputation wasn't of the best. He watched as attendants dragged the injured man from the ring.

'Who won the main bout?'

'Sutton. I think it was a fix.'

'Naturally.' Lacey heaved himself into a more comfortable position. His suit was rumpled and his shirt stained with perspiration. His nails needed a manicure and his hair a trim but he had his uses. He was a leech hanging close to those with money. A fixer and pander, tout and provider. A high-priced errand boy with ambitions. 'And the rest?'

Atwater mouthed his cigar. 'The usual. All deadly boring for the most part.' You posturing bastard, though Lacey, but he retained his smile. Spitefully he said, 'I thought you'd be at Cybele's party. Aren't you interested in the comet?'

'I've seen the comet and I didn't choose to go.'

His tone betrayed him. He hadn't been invited and Lacey knew it. He also knew why. Atwater had nothing but money and not enough of that to interest the Pent Crowd. He lacked the right connections and the right background. He wasn't entertaining, stimulating, beautiful or intellectual. He was also old. Lacey hoped he was vulnerable.

He thought he was but a man couldn't be too careful. Not dealing with a sadistic swine like Atwater. He felt sweat dew his palms and recognised the signs of nervousness. Well, he had reason to be nervous. One wrong move and it would be his last.

Casually he nodded towards the ring where boxers fought with spiked gloves, blood running over their naked bodies. 'Ever thought of taking it up yourself? There's quite a thrill in feeling teeth against your knuckles.'

Atwater puffed at his cigar and made no reply.

'Of course, there's something better. A whole lot better. All the fun and none of the struggle.'

'Such as?'

Lacey's smile was enigmatic. 'Can't you guess?'

'Dope?' Atwater snorted his contempt. 'To be good it's got to be strong and I'm not fool enough to get myself hooked on a habit. Do I look like a man who wants to be a cripple?'

'No, Frank, but you're talking about the wrong stuff.'

'The soft drugs? Pot, the amphetamines, Benzedrine and other stimulants? They are for kids.'

Lacey surreptitiously wiped the palms of his hands. Did the guy have to be so dumb? Make it so hard? Almost he was tempted to let the matter drop but the fish was close to the hook and might swallow the bait.

Quietly he said, 'Try again, Frank.'

'L.S.D., then. An acid trip to nowhere.' Atwater shook his head. 'I've tried it and it's a waste of time. Some of those cerebral meanderings led straight into nightmare. When I take a trip want to be sure it's going to be fun.'

Lacey drew a deep breath. This was it. The hit. The big moment. 'Maybe you used the wrong vehicle,' he said meaning-fully. 'I'm not talking about acid — who wants to blow a gasket? But there's something else. It's harmless and works like a dream. You may have heard of it. Word gets around.'

Atwater looked at the ash on his cigar. 'And you have access?'

'I've got connections. You want it, I can get it.'

At a price, of course, but that was to be expected, nothing in the world was free. But, if half of what he'd heard was true, there wasn't enough money to buy all it could give you. And why not try it for once? Once couldn't hurt and what had he to lose? The bouts were getting trite;

people fighting with knives and clubs, women and men getting abused as a penalty for defeat. He was getting bored and what else was there to do?

'All right,' he said. 'Why not?'

5

The oil was warm, scented with roses, smooth with the tactile impact of rippling silk. Sutton relaxed as he lay supine on the couch, letting the masseur do his job, eyes closed as he retreated into a private world. It was a good world in which everyone was kind and respectful and polite. A world in which he was not accepted as being a normal part w a normal part. A place in which he tru belonged. It was good to lie and drift and feel recent tensions unwind.

'A good fight, Mr. Sutton.' The masseur was a slim man with liquid eyes and overdeveloped hands. They rested on the oiled skin, hard, firm, thumbs probing, fingertips like blunt claws as they raked away strain and fatigue. 'You displayed a real mastery of technique and muscular control.'

'You saw it?'

'I was permitted to watch, Mr. Sutton.

I had a small bet on your skill and my tailor should thank you for the custom I will bring him.'

He was talking too much, breaking the valued introspection, and tiny muscles tensed in unspoken protest. The masseur recognised the signs and fell silent as he continued his work.

Sensuous, thought Sutton with a vague detachment. Oil as warm as the lips of a loving woman. Firm hands winning a response from jaded flesh yet, while firm, they were gentle. He relaxed even more. It was good to lie and feel the firm yet insidious pressure of the hands and the smooth caress of the oil. Better to have walked from the ring, sweating, nostrils filled with the rank odour of blood, ears numbed with the rearing adulation of the crowd. To walk and not be carried. To have won instead of having lost.

'You are growing tense, Mr. Sutton,' said the masseur quietly. 'It is important that you continue to relax.'

He was right, of course, thinking about the past was never a wise thing to do. The fight was over, done with, a thing accomplished. Yet he found it oddly hard to retreat into his private world. Now he was the champion. It made a difference.

Oil, he thought as the masseur applied more of the scented fluid. What was so special about oil? With it kings were anointed by their people. Civilisations had used it to fill lamps with which to light their way. Babies had been cleaned with it. Considerate husbands used it with their frigid wives. Machines used it.

Machines used it all the time.

Like fighters.

Did that make him a machine?

Suddenly irritable he opened his eyes and sat upright on the couch. The masseur stepped back, eyes reproachful, hands still flexed as if they could still feel the firm contours of oiled and naked flesh.

'I haven't yet finished, Mr. Sutton.' The masseur had a light-brown skin and over-waved hair. 'I have yet to fully ease the bicuspids and — '

'Forget it.' Sutton reached for a cigarette and inhaled with careless indifference. 'I've had enough. Hand me my wallet.'

He took the pigskin, counted out money, added more for a tip and thrust the notes into the open palm.

'Thank you, Mr. Sutton. May I wish you the very best of good fortune now that you have gained the crown?'

'Why not?' Good wishes were better than cursed. 'And thank you for your trouble.'

'It was a pleasure. I'll be happy to rub you down whenever you wish Mr. Sutton. I am really quite good at my profession.'

Perhaps too damn good! Sutton dragged at his cigarette and felt smoke bite his lungs as he watched the masseur leave the cubicle. Educated, proud, acutely aware of his social inferiority. Such a man could get his revenge in subtle ways. The skilful transfer of areas of erotic sensitivity, for example. In such a case a man would no longer wholly enjoy the caresses of a normal woman. Perhaps he was a queen working to build up later custom. Sutton shrugged. In the Game you met all kinds.

He leaned back, smoking, looking at the wall. The cubicle held the couch, a locker, a washbasin and small table and two chairs. Once it had been a dressing room in the theatre that now held the stadium. A small, private theatre with soundproofed walls and barred doors. Most cities had them.

The cigarette crackled a little as he sucked smoke through the filter, the tip glowing like a miniature furnace, dulling beneath its coating of ash. Swinging his legs over the edge of the couch he stood upright, six feet eight inches of tempered bone and muscle, his features hard, classical beneath the short nap of his hair. Thin lines traced a pattern on his chest, stomach and arms. Old scars from his early days while he was still learning how to handle a knife.

He turned as the cubicle door swung open. Fred Lomax entered without knocking. He was a middle-aged man with a harassed face and a too-young suit. He stared at the nude fighter and saw the cigarette.

'Are you crazy, Sutton? Kill the butt!'

Sutton said a foul word. It didn't shake the agent.

'Listen,' he said. 'If you want to take a

chance then go bare-handed against blades, but why do it the slow way? Kill the butt. You're in training and lungs cost money.'

Sutton dropped the cigarette and trod on it. The coal burned his bare foot but his face remained impassive. Life had taught him that. When hurt keep it to yourself. No one has time for a whiner.

'Talking about money,' he said. 'What have I got coming?

'A handful of centuries.' Lomax became effusive. 'Big, money, boy! Didn't I say that if you stuck with me we'd get rich?'

'You did,' agreed Sutton coldly. 'But you didn't say who was going to get all the money. Five hundred isn't enough.'

'How do you figure that?'

'The odds were good. Fives I wouldn't draw in thirty. I did. Twos I wouldn't get the crown. I did. I told you to put it all on the line. Why didn't you?'

Lomax coughed.

'I'm waiting. The fight was worth a clear thousand. As I see it there should be thirteen coming if you'd done as I said.'

'And if you hadn't drawn at twenty-six?'

57

Lomax tilted his head as he stared up at the fighter. 'Now you listen to me, boy. First I get my cut and pay expenses, right? Then I've got to play it safe. Suppose you had got all cut up? Without my money how would you pay the medical bills?'

'I don't know,' said Sutton bleakly. 'Maybe I thought that you'd be willing to protect your investment.' Quietly he added, 'Are you holding out on me, Fred?'

'Now, boy, would I do a thing like that?'

'Don't call me 'boy'.'

'All right, Denis. But would I?'

Sutton was ironic. 'Sure. All the time.'

'Not this time,' insisted Lomax. He was sweating. 'Listen. You know the fix was in and you certain to win the crown. If I'd backed you heavy the odds would have fallen and it would have been noticed. The Syndicate wouldn't have liked it and you'd be out of favour. Is that what you want?'

'I want seven thousand five hundred dollars. How you get it is your business. But get it — or get out!'

'I'm you agent, boy. Your manager. You

figure on telling me where to go?' Lomax narrowed his eyes. 'Now you just open up your ears. Talk big and you'll end weeping. How would you like a shot of acid in the eyes? Or maybe a cut sciatic nerve? Fighters are ten a penny and don't you forget it.'

Sutton looked down at his hands. They were steady but, all over his body, he could feel the twitch of muscles tensing in anger. Quietly he said, 'What's the pitch? The champion's down, when do I follow?'

'Now you're talking sense.' Lomax relaxed, smiling. 'The Syndicate figure you good for another half-dozen bouts. You win five and the odds will be right the time after. Let him draw in twenty and win in under the ton. The payoff will be enough to keep you for life.'

'Sure,' said Sutton dryly. 'If I don't live too long. Is this what you call the big time?'

Lomax shrugged. 'Hell, kid, don't blame me. I'm just as you are. A cog in the machine.'

'All right,' said Sutton. 'You don't have to explain.'

'That's my boy!' Lomax was relieved. He'd said too much and was regretting it but what the hell? The kid would play along if he knew what was good for him. 'Now I've got a bonus for you. Something nice. A bit of paying fun to go with the crown.' He took a slip of paper from his pocket. 'She sent this down with a fifty-dollar bill but that was just for the messenger. Play it right and you should make several centuries. Maybe more.'

He grew expansive. 'And it's all yours. I don't want a cent.'

Sutton took the paper and looked at the address, the instructions it contained. 'Is she young?'

Lomax shrugged. 'I don't know, but what the hell does it matter?'

She wasn't young. Her hair was false and her face was raddled beneath the paint and she bore the marks of cosmetic surgery but she was rich and had the arrogance of wealth. Even so she was polite.

'It's good for you to have come, Denis. Did anyone see you?'

He shook his head as he entered the

apartment. The lights were low and the air scented with musk. The carpets rose to his ankles and the walls were covered with genuine silk. Through an open door he could see the loom of a wide bed covered with soft fabrics. On the embroidered silk lay the braided thong of a riding crop.

'Would you care for a drink?'

He nodded, watching as she poured two glasses almost full of sparkling champagne. She wore stockings, a suspender belt and brassiere beneath a loose kimono. High-heeled slippers added inches to her height. She was not a woman who intended to waste any time.

'Have you been fighting long?' She handed him one of the glasses and looked at him over the rim of her own. Her eyes were bright and the touch of her hand was febrile. She was keyed up and ready to go, an emotional bomb held barely in check.

'Long enough.' He sipped and remembered to smile.

'But you look so young!' The robe opened as she stooped towards him. 'So terribly young.' Then she added, 'All but your eyes. They've seen too much pain. Too much blood.' The tip of her tongue moved wetly across the swell of her lower lip. 'It must be wonderfully exciting to stand there in front of all those people and do what you do.'

'Fight,' he said. 'Cut. Maim.' He took another sip of his champagne. 'I do it for the money.'

'You'd do anything for money, wouldn't you?'

'That's right.'

He stripped, throwing aside his clothing and standing naked, his skin a rich, warm velvet in the soft lighting. He saw the widening of her eyes, the ragged inhalation of her breath.

'My God,' she said. 'You looked good in the ring but you look better now, you big black — '

He felt the rage, the seething turmoil of emotion no white person could ever understand, the overwhelming combination of triumph, contempt and the desire for revenge born of his youth and the things that had been done to him, the way he'd been forced to live. To eat dirt and turn away and always to remember that even supposed white friends were only acting that way because they gained a personal satisfaction from being liberal. The gushing friends who tried so hard. Who tried too hard and made it so obvious they patronised, and, for him, gratitude was something he had never felt obligated to own.

'Darling!' she breathed. 'You big, beautiful black darling!'

Her nails dug deep as she led him towards the bedroom and the waiting lash. The braided thing whistled as it cut the air.

'Down,' she said thickly. 'On the bed!'

The soft fabrics rose around him, the pillow closing about his face, blinding, smothering with softness and memories. The sharp sting of the whip caused him to jerk and the sweat to slime his face.

The pain of the whip was a needle stabbing at his brain.

He could stand it as he had stood it before consoling himself with thoughts of the money he was earning. But this time it wasn't the same. Now he was the champion and for what? To be beaten for an old slut's perverted lust. To be threatened and used, fixed and manipulated by the Syndicate. To know that he was going to be cut and crippled and thrown aside. Would this white trash want him then? Would anyone?

And where was his pride?

He rolled, falling from the bed, rising to snatch the whip from the woman's hand. His left hand clamped on the back of her neck and he threw her to the bed, prone, her face buried in the pillows. Against the silk her body moved like a soft, white slug, the bands of suspender belt and brassiere thin strips of darkness. Stockinged legs jerked as he brought down the lash.

'Don't!' She screamed, rising, fighting the pressure of his hands. 'For God's sake! Don't!'

He pressed down, hard, muffling her cries in the smothering pillow as his right arm plied the whip.

The screams had excited him, filling his head with the pounding rush of blood and drawing his lips back in a grimace of rage. Now, by God, she was going to get it. Get a taste of what it all meant. To be on the receiving end for a change instead of dishing it out. Her and all those like her, the Syndicate, the white supremacists, the cheaters and stealers and gougers and users of the world!

Anger fed the strength of his arm and sent the lash whistling spitefully through the air to land with a meaty splat on the writhing body. Red weals grew, tracing a pattern over the buttocks, the thighs, the broad back. They deepened, broke the skin, became dewed with glistening droplets of blood.

It was some time before he realised that the woman was dead.

6

Ralph Mancini lived high in a block of ten-year old apartments constructed to appeal to those who liked comfort, space and security. The main room was three hundred feet square, the bedroom half as large, the study a little smaller. There was a kitchen and bathroom containing both shower and tub. Glass walls gave an unrestricted view of the city and a heliport occupied the roof.

An attendant touched the brim of his cap as Ralph headed for the elevator. 'Good evening, Major Mancini. It's a fine, clear night.'

'Very clear,' said Ralph, entering the cage.

'But to be expected after such a nice day.'

'Very nice,' said Ralph, pressing the button.

Neither was being wholly truthful. Joe Connors had aching feet, worrying debts and had discovered that morning that his thirteen-year old daughter was three months pregnant. Ralph had spent the day chasing rainbows and was hungry, tired and irritable.

He heard the music as he opened the door of his apartment. Stravinsky's Rite of Spring, one of Lavinia's favourites from his collection. The stereophonic held undiluted perfection and he stood, leaning back against the door, eyes closed as he relished the majestic cadences.

'Is that you Ralph?'

Lavinia was his wife this month and he opened his eyes as she stepped from the kitchen. She wore a simple dress reaching almost to her knees, the soft fabric taut over hips and thighs, moulding itself to the yielding contours of her breasts. Her hair was a rich brown neatly coiffed to form a frame for her wide-eyed face, the nose endearing because of its slight imperfection. Her lips were full and she smelt of lavender.

They kissed and she stepped back, her eyes holding concern.

'You look tired, darling. Have a hard day?'

'A tiresome one.'

'And no sleep, I bet.'

'No,' he admitted. 'I went straight from the party to the office and changed there. Since then I've been beating my head against a wall.' He didn't explain and she didn't question. 'And you?'

'The usual.' She poured him a drink as he sat down. It was Vermouth laced with vodka and spiked with a touch of lime, his normal before-dinner cocktail. 'A little shopping. A little housework. Some sewing and reading. You know how it is.'

'No,' he said. 'But I can guess.'

'Woman's work.' Her hand was soft as it touched his cheek. 'I've got steaks, pork chops, liver and kidneys. Could you go for a big mixed grill?'

'That and anything else you've got around. I haven't eaten all day.'

'A man like you needs meat,' she said. 'And a lot of it. I'll start your bath while you finish your drink. We can eat right afterwards.'

He relaxed as she moved away, enjoying the comfort of his home and the woman who shared it, wondering a little what the next one would be like. Some things he knew. She would be between 5 feet 6 and 5 feet 8 because he didn't like his women to be very short or very tall. She would weigh about 135 pounds because he didn't like them to be either too thin or too plump. She would be able to play chess and would share his interests in music and literature. Her age would be about 25 and she would be a good cook and completely satisfying as to his sexual needs. She would be honest, trustworthy and faithful.

The agency guaranteed it.

Soaking in the tub, the scented water lapping at his chin, he thought of some previous ones he had known. Clarissa, the one before Lavinia, had been a blonde. Mary had been a redhead. Sylvia had come from Mexico and had taught him how to savour tequila. Margarite had been Afro-American and Lallia had come from the Caribbean. Their faces swam before him, growing vague as they receded in time, losing their importance in the dilution of others. It was easier to think of Lavinia.

'Ralph?'

He jerked, realising that he had almost fallen asleep, the water splashing as he moved.

'I'll be there in a minute.'

'You've got five. I'm just going to make the salad.'

With chives, of course, and sliced peppers and the merest suspicion of garlic. He would remember Lavinia for her salads if for nothing else.

The doorbell chimed as they ended the meal with coffee in the lounge. Lavinia rose and went to the door. When she returned she was smiling.

'There's someone to see you, dear. A minister. The Reverend Edwin Carslake.'

'A minister?'

'That's what he said.'

Frowning Ralph went to the door and looked through the peephole. The hundred and eighty degree lens showed the passage to be clear on either side of the benign figure standing beyond the panel. He was a man of about sixty with a large head, old-fashioned spectacles and a thin neck embraced by the traditional dog collar. He wore a dark hat and suit and carried a small leather-bound book, obviously a bible.

Ralph spoke into the grille. 'You wanted to see me?'

'If you would be so good as to spare me a little of your valuable time.'

Ralph hesitated then opened the door. It was late but the man was old and alone and the guards would have checked his credentials. He removed his hat as he entered the apartment, revealing a balding head, which gleamed in the light as he made a small bow to where Lavinia sat on the couch.

'Good evening, my dear. I trust that I am causing you no inconvenience?'

'None,' said Lavinia. 'Will you sit? Have coffee?'

'Thank you.' Carslake sipped at the coffee, his adam's apple bobbing in his scrawny throat. His knuckles were swollen with arthritis but his eyes held the alert twinkle of youth. Putting down the empty cup he dabbed at his lips with a handkerchief. 'I should explain that I am the incumbent of St. Marthas on

Freemont Avenue. Perhaps you know it?'

'The progressive Church of the New Commandment.' Lavinia nodded, 'I know it.'

'A small Church but growing from strength to strength and can you guess why?' Carslake held up one hand as if he were in a pulpit. 'I will tell you why. It is because we have returned to the fundamental basis of the faith as directed by the Holy bible. We have shed false dogma and the hypocrisy and evil blindness that has hidden the True Word for so many generations. I must be humble but it is hard not to feel pride at the happiness and comfort we have brought to so many. Together we are forming a new spiritual birth, which will expand to encompass the world. These are evil times, my friends. Death and terror stalk our streets and the hearts of men are hardened against their fellows but, soon, all will change and again the lion shall lie down at peace with the lamb. And do you know why? It is because we have returned to the Original Teaching. We practise the New Commandment. The logos on which the faith is founded. The rock on which we must build if the world is to be saved from the evil fury of Armageddon. The rock is love, my friends. Love!'

Ralph blinked at the evangelical fervour.

'How can I hope to describe the tremendous uplifting of the spirit which comes to all who embrace the revitalised faith? The calm and tranquillity? The perfect communion of heart and mind in the all-encasing love of the Divine? I cannot. Words cannot convey that miraculous transformation. You must experience it for yourselves and see the radiance on the faces of others as they meet, one with the other, at our weekly agapes. Then — '

Ralph interrupted. 'Agapes?'

'Love feasts held by the early Christians,' said Lavinia quietly. 'They were condemned by the Council of Carthage in 397.'

'Misguided men who yielded to the machinations of Satan,' said Carslake. 'They gave themselves to the direct instructions of the Lord. For did not he say, 'I give you the commandment. Love one another. As I have loved you, so you are to love one another.' You will find it in the Gospel of St. John. Chapter 13, verse 34.'

'You quote a pretty high authority,' said Ralph dryly. 'Does it really say that?'

'The Bible is here and you can check for yourself, my friend.' Carslake lifted the leather-bound volume. 'The commandment is the direct word of Our Lord. We are to love each other. St. Paul emphasizes the matter. In Romans, 13;10, he says 'Love your neighbour as yourself. Love cannot wrong a neighbour, therefore love is the fulfilling of the law. You are interested in fulfilling the law?'

Ralph smiled at the question. 'Of course.'

'Then you should participate in our activities. I assure you, my friends, that the agapes of the Progressive Church of the New Commandment are countenanced and directed by Holy Writ.'

Lavinia poured more coffee. 'You make it sound very interesting, Reverend. There can't be very much wrong with the concept of love.'

'My child, how right you are! Truly, 'from the mouths of babes come forth words of wisdom'.' Carslake leaned forward where he sat, his eyes bright with religious fervour. 'To love is to obey the command of the Lord as set forth in the Holy Book. The message is plain and often repeated. In the Gospel of St. John Chapter 4, verse 18, he says, 'There is no fear in love', and in verse 8, he says, 'He that does not love does not know God; for God is love!' I could continue for the evidence is so plain. Matthew 22:37. Psalm 119:165. Leviticus 19:18. The first epistle of St. Peter 3:8. All speak of the necessity of love.'

'I agree with you,' said Ralph. 'But what happens at the agapes of yours? Do a lot of people just stand around loving each other?'

'Not stand around, my friend,' beamed Carslake. 'We obey the New Commandment implicitly. I cannot tell you how popular our services have become and, of course, there are smaller occasions where groups of the faithful gather to find a closer fulfilment.' He rose and produced a handful of papers from an inside pocket. 'I will leave you these tracts and I do so hope, my friends, that you will come and join our happy community.'

Lavinia smiled as Ralph returned from showing out their caller. 'Well, are you converted?'

'To love? My dear, you converted me the first moment I say you.'

'To his church, stupid! You know what these agapes are, I suppose?'

'You told me. Love feast.'

'In the literal sense of the word. It's a gimmick so that the sex-starved can get what they want under the cloak of Higher Authority. If they don't burn down his Church our reverend friend should do well.'

'So it's a racket?' Ralph felt an odd disappointment. Carslake had seemed so genuine. 'I should have guessed as much.'

Lavinia shook her head. 'Wrong. It's no racket. He is a genuine minister of religion and his church is a registered organisation. It's just that those who join his congregation are looking for a little more than the love of God. They are after the love of each other. It's basically a wife-swap club prettied up with fancy trimmings. And, before you get any ideas, I couldn't go if you wanted me to. It's against the contract.'

Ralph poured himself more coffee and stood, sipping it as he looked down at the woman. Tonight she had revealed unsuspected depths.

'You knew,' he said. 'About the agapes, I mean. I never thought you were religious.'

'I've read the Bible,' she said. 'And I know a little about it. Enough to know that you can prove almost anything you want to by selecting favourable references.' She lifted her arms, smiling, the action drawing the material of the dress taut over her breasts. 'He thought we were married,' she said. 'Interested in spreading our wings a little.'

'You can't blame him,' he said quietly. 'We look the part.'

'Hungry for others?'

'Married. You seem to fit this place. As if you belonged.'

She lowered her arms, smiling, looking

wonderful against the rich fabric of the couch. 'We get on well together,' she admitted. 'I felt at home here from the very first. Almost as if I knew exactly where everything was. It wasn't a bit like some of the other places I've been to when — '

He was harsh. 'Forget it! I don't want to hear about any of the others!'

'Ralph?' Her hand caught his arm, held it as he set down the unfinished cup of coffee. 'Is something wrong?'

'No.' He sat beside her, a little ashamed of his outburst, his lack of self-control. 'It's just that I'm tired,' he explained. 'A little irritable and our recent guest didn't help. I hate to be preached to.'

'Would you like to go to bed, dear?'

'Not yet.' He rose and poured a drink, brandy mixed with rum, the Pent Crowd's latest tipple. He lifted the glass as he called to Lavinia. 'Want one?'

'Yes, please, darling.'

Always agreeable, he thought as he poured her drink. Always ready to share, to understand and to participate. If he wanted to get stinking drunk then she would ride along with him. The perfect wife.

'Don't you ever get tired of it?' He returned to the couch, drinks in his hands. 'All this changing about. This moving from one place to another month after month.' He saw her eyes as he handed her the glass. They were watchful, cautious, the eyes of a suspect about to be interrogated, wanting to please the questioner but wishing that he wouldn't question at all. 'I'm sorry. I know there some things we shouldn't talk about. Forget I asked.'

'It isn't too bad,' she said, ignoring his last remark, knowing that he wanted to make conversation. 'The agency is one of the best and careful whom they take on as clients. It's just like a job really. No,' she corrected, 'it is a job. And a good one. I'm rarely bored. I like housework and shopping and being a wife. A month is long enough to get to know someone and yet not long enough to get to hate them. Sometimes things aren't just as you'd like them to be and then you console yourself that it isn't going to last for long. It's like a continuous new-start. A perpetual honeymoon.'

That's from her side, he thought. And from mine? Much the same. A new, stimulating companion at the beginning of each month. A constant change. Thoughtfully he sipped his drink wondering at his inner turmoil, his unusual restlessness. The visitor, he guessed, and is natural assumption that he was speaking to a normally married couple. Lavinia had certainly looked and acted the part. He wondered if he could bear to see her locked in an embrace with another man.

And then wondered why he was annoyed at the thought the concept aroused.

Lavinia put down her empty glass. 'Would you like another?'

'No thank you.'

'Then let's go to bed,' she said decisively. 'You look all in and I'm not having my man sleep on a couch.'

Later, between the cool sheets, his hand reached out to grip her own.

'Darling,' he said. 'I love you.'

Her hand returned the pressure.

'And I love you too, darling. You know that.'

'I mean it,' he insisted. 'I really mean it.'

Her hand lay quiescent.

'I know you do darling. And so do I.'

A mechanical response? Play acting to fit the part she was employed to fill? They had spoken of love before, often, both during the heat of passion and afterwards to feed again the flames of desire. And each time the words had been genuine and sincerely spoken — while the moment lasted. But did she mean anything else? And how often had she said similar things before?

She was about twenty-five, which made it a maximum of seven years. Add a few more before she'd joined the agency and call it a hundred. A hundred different men she had enjoyed what he had just experienced. He turned, restless, annoyed with his train of thought. So what if she'd had so many? Many of the women running with the Pent Crowd clocked up a higher score during a season. And, anyway, what the hell did it matter?

7

Ralph woke late the next morning and hurried breakfast while Lavinia phoned for a cab. She clung to him briefly as they kissed on parting, then pushed him firmly towards the door.

'Be home early,' she ordered. 'And don't you dare eat too much. I'm cooking a special dinner for tonight.'

He hesitated. 'Why special?'

'Because I want to, silly! Now, move!'

The cabbie cursed as he manoeuvred his vehicle through the litter still cluttering the streets from the previous night's demonstrations. Broken glass, trash cans and accumulated garbage lay heaped on the edge of the pavement where cleaning gangs had swept it. Burned automobiles rested in smouldering heaps.

'Damn kids! The trouble is they've too much money and too much time. If I have my way I'd shove the lot of them into the army.'

'We've no conscription,' reminded Ralph. 'Anyway, why should the army be saddled with them?'

'It'd make something of them, that's why.' The driver swore as he came to a diversion. 'And so what if we haven't got conscription? We don't need it. Just pass a law kicking them in. We've got enough laws, one more won't make that much difference!' He swore again, stamping on his brakes. 'What the hell's wrong now?'

Cars jammed the pavement at an intersection where crowds gathered on the sidewalks. They moved slowly and purposefully across the street ignoring the whistles of policemen and their shouted commands. Ralph looked to either side. Discarded placards and banners lay crumpled and broken on the street. As he watched a girl picked one up and held it defiantly over her head. The wording was daubed in black paint.

BEAT BIG BROTHER!

'Trust them to cause trouble.' The driver sat back, fuming as he lit a cigarette. It was against the law for him to smoke while on duty but he didn't seem to worry about that. 'That's all the creeps ever do, cause trouble. What the hell we got to have laws to govern things, haven't we? Then why can't they obey them like everyone else?'

Ralph looked at the girl. She was young, attractive, neatly dressed. A junior secretary, probably, on her way to the office. She seemed to have nothing in common with the usual deadhead crowd with their dark blue denim trousers and tunics. The coolie style, accentuated by short pigtails for both sexes, so that it was almost impossible to tell them apart. So why had she taken it on herself to join the protest?

The cab moved forward, stopped again as a flood of people surged across the street just ahead. They crossed from one side to the other, moving in a circle around the intersection, freezing the traffic in mounting jams.

'The dumb, lazy sleazy bastards!' The driver was blowing his top. 'Why the hell don't they toe the line? We're too easy with them, that's what. Back in the last century Hitler would have known how to deal with them. He had places for crumbs like this.'

Ralph studied his face in the rear-view mirror. The driver was red-faced, angry, his cheeks mottled. About forty, Ralph guessed. Lacking any first-hand experience of war.

'Hitler would have settled them,' said the driver. 'He wouldn't have let them gum up the works the way they're doing now. He had the right idea.'

'Sure,' said Ralph dryly. 'Toe the line or else. Would you like to live under a dictatorship?'

'What's in a name? Sometimes it takes a strong guy to get things done. Look at the roads he built, the houses. That guy was a genius.'

And you would like to serve such a man, thought Ralph. You'd like to wear the uniform and carry the whip and give the orders. He turned again to stare through the window. On the sidewalk a middle-aged man was arguing with a sweating officer.

'Look, I want to cross the road,' he was saying. 'For Christ's sake, haven't I got a right to cross the goddam road!'

'You wait until I say you can!' The officer pressed him back. 'You stand in line and wait.'

'What the hell for?' The man was angry. 'I'm late as it is. The traffic's stopped and others are crossing. Why the hell can't I join them?'

'So you can come back again?' The officer shoved again, harder. 'You crumbs make me sick. You think you're smart jamming the traffic flow? You think I don't know what you're doing? You wait until I tell you to move.'

'To hell with that! I'm goddam well going to cross the goddam road and you goddam well aren't going to stop me!'

'That's what you think.' The officer grabbed the man as he blew his whistle. 'Take this one in,' he said as other officers came running. 'Book him for conspiracy, conduct likely to cause a breach of the peace and for obstructing an officer in the course of his duty.' He turned and glared at the cab. 'All right, get moving, force your way through.'

The driver sucked in his breath as the

cab rolled forward.

'That's the sprit! That old coot'll think twice before he joins up with another bunch of deadheads. A guy like that should've had more sense.'

Ralph was curious. 'How would you have handled the situation back there?'

'Simple.' The driver blew smoke. 'If I was a cop I'd give one warning and then the signal. If anyone got himself run down I'd book him for disobedience.'

'That's a new one,' said Ralph. 'Is there such a law?'

'If there isn't there should be.' The cabbie spun his wheel. 'The 20th precinct, you said?'

'That's right.'

'You a cop or something.'

'Something,' said Ralph. 'Now quit talking and keep your mind on the road.'

The real work of the United Nations Law Enforcement Agency was conducted well away from the gas-factory on lower Manhattan. The 20th Precinct was a new building, partly given over to the local police and courts, mostly filled with the giant UNLEA computers, offices and staff. There was plenty of room. The place was almost as large as Dexter Prison and, in many ways, resembled it.

Thelma looked up as Ralph entered his office. The secretary was prim, tight-mouthed, devoid of humour. She said, 'Good morning, Major. Colonel Pryor left word that he would like to see you at noon. Captain Markham has reported sick. Mrs. Hickstead is waiting in your office.'

'Who is she?'

'An attorney. She is replacing Mr. Nicholls. Colonel Pryor thought it would be a good idea if you were to show her around and act as liaison for a few hours. Captain Markham would have done it, but as I told you, he has reported sick.'

Ralph nodded. 'Did the run-through I ordered come down from the computers yet?'

'Not yet, Major. I will do my best to expedite the matter.'

'You do that,' said Ralph, and went into his inner room.

Mrs. Hickstead was a woman of about thirty, tall, slim, refreshingly well-groomed.

She wore a simple suit of dark material, dark stockings and shoes of black leather. Her hands were delicately boned and bore only the two rings on the third finger of her left hand. Her hair was dark and neatly cropped about her head. She rose as Ralph entered the room, smiling as he extended her hand.

'Major Mancini?'

'Ralph. How is Max? Not ill, I hope?'

'Mr. Nicholls has withdrawn from the group. I am taking his place.'

Ralph caught the subtle inflection, the hint of disapproval and inwardly sighed. He said, 'Max did a lot of good work, Mrs. Hickstead. But even the most dedicated of us can sometimes weary of beating his head against a wall.'

'Hilda,' she said, and smiled. 'If we are to be informal it has to be mutual.'

'Hilda, then. You condemn him?'

'I have no right to do that,' she said precisely. 'It's just that there are so many people who need our help and — '

'You think he should have stuck to the grindstone and not concerned himself with building up his own practice?' Ralph shook his head. 'Even the most dedicated have to keep an eye on their own welfare, Hilda. Max was running himself into the ground and he knew it. Another few months and he'd have lost the last of his legitimate clients.'

'Legitimate?'

'Individual, then. Your profession is not too happy at the way you conduct your business and neither are lucrative clients. But you must know that and it isn't my problem. Your husband's perhaps, but not mine.'

'Nor his,' she said flatly. 'We were divorced two years ago.'

'I'm sorry.'

'Why should you be? It happens all the time.' She shook herself as if shedding unpleasant memories. 'Shall we get on with our business?'

They were waiting in a line-up room, a hundred and twelve of them, sitting in the narrow seats facing the rostrum. Young for the most part, the majority wearing the deadhead uniform, dark blue shadows with white, brown and black faces. A few older ones sat in mental isolation, their clothing rumpled and stained. A pale-faced, distraught man rose as Ralph and the woman entered.

'Say, who can I speak to around here? I'm innocent and — '

'Sit down,' rapped a guard.

'But — '

'Sit down!'

He slumped as Ralph leaned towards the attorney. 'This is last night's collection,' he said quietly. 'Those who have your card or who want legal representation. You can act for them or not as you wish.'

'I'll take them,' she said. 'All of them.'

A glutton for punishment, thought Ralph, but she would learn. Not that it made any difference, he knew, but the formalities had to be observed and if she wanted to wear herself out that was her privilege. Like Max she might decide that she was on a one-way street to nowhere and, like him, she might decide to quit. He hoped so. She was too much of a woman to waste.

'Normally you'll be working with Captain Markham,' he said. 'He will process the cases and put them in the picture. The charge sheets and details of arrest are here.' He touched a pile of documents. 'If you want to wade through them individually that is your privilege but it will be a waste of time.'

'I don't see that,' she protested. 'How am I going to defend my clients unless I am well-briefed?'

'It isn't a question of defence,' he said. 'It is a matter of you pleading mitigation. And we're all pushed for time. That is why we use this system, it makes things a lot easier.'

Rising he looked at the rows of watching faces 'It is my duty as presiding officer, to inform you of your legal duties. Under the United Nations Drug Offences Act of it is an offence to be in possession of any prescribed drug and, in this case, 'possession' means to have on or in the person. There are a hundred and eighty-two signatory countries to this Act which supersedes and rationalises all previous national legislation. All of you here are guilty of an offence against the act and this guilt has been proven by the medical tests, which show the presence of drugs in your bodies. You are, however, entitled to legal representation. Those who want it may stand.'

All but a dozen reared to their feet, the pale-faced man among them.

'I'm innocent,' he shouted. 'I'm under medical treatment!'

Hilda looked at him. 'Are you a member of Defence?'

'No, but I'll join. I'll join right away if you'll let me!'

Twenty dollars, a card, the right to call on skill and brains and legal help at any time of the day or night. A scheme to provide those who thought they might need it with the insurance of a lawyer. A good idea, Ralph admitted, but how was it used? To help fools get themselves out of the trouble they went out of their way to find. And, in the majority of cases, a complete waste of time. No wonder Max had quit.

He looked to where the woman was making out a form. If the man had the money she would give him ten times as much value in return. If he didn't she would carry him. She was that kind of woman.

'Get his name,' he said to a guard. 'The phone number and details of his doctor. Check it out and if he's clean let him go.'

'No,' said Hilda sharply. 'You can't do that. He's been charged and must be tried. There could even be a case for wrongful arrest.'

'I'm trying to help you,' he said patiently. 'Save you trouble and expense. These characters will say anything if they think there's a hope in hell of getting away with it. Maybe he's telling the truth and maybe not. He could even have a phoney doctor fixed to give him an out. And let's not have any talk of wrongful arrest. He's guilty under the Act until he proves himself innocent.'

'Then why didn't you check his story earlier? Why hold him at all?'

'It isn't our job to prove them innocent. If the tests are positive that's all we worry about. The rest is up to them.' He felt a momentary annoyance as he saw her expression. 'It's his own fault. He should have carried a document from his doctor saying what he was prescribed, how much and when it had to be taken. Damn it, Hilda, we aren't nurses to wipe their noses. The problem's too big for that.'

'It seems that it's too big for a lot of things,' she said coldly. 'The law was designed to protect the individual. To seem to be using it as an instrument against them.'

'As I understand it the law is designed to protect society,' he said flatly. 'And please remember that I didn't make it, I just carry it out. Now, as for the rest of your clients. It is your right to plead their cases individually if you wish but, if you will take my advice, you'll treat them as a unit. The court will appreciate your cooperation and be more inclined to listen to you when you have a genuine defence. With this bunch you haven't. They've already been questioned and those who cooperated are known. Those who refused to give assistance are noted as being intractable.'

'Another abrogation of their rights,' she said. 'It isn't a crime to refuse to talk.'

He looked at her with a hint of

amusement. 'You haven't been in practise very long, have you?'

'What has that got to do with it?'

'Nothing, but the law as practised isn't the same as you read in books. Theoretically, perhaps, but not in reality. There isn't time and the usual transgressor hasn't the money to buy experienced representation. So we take short cuts and make deals. If someone cooperates they get it a little easier than those who don't. And surely you must have heard of 'silent contempt'?'

'Of course.' She looked at the rows of men and girl, still patiently standing. 'What's going to happen to them?'

'For first offenders three months. For second offenders, six, and third timers get a year. After that it is how the court sees fit.'

'A lot of people,' she said. 'And a lot of time. What happens when you've nowhere to put then?'

'That's simple,' he said. 'We build more prisons.'

8

Leaving Hilda with her clients Ralph made his way to one of the interrogation rooms. This was more of Markham's work but it was basically simple and it was easier to do it himself than to find someone else. UNLEA men were always hard-pushed and there where never enough hours in any single day.

'Seven.' Lieutenant Merrow passed over a clipboard containing the details. 'All four-time losers. All on the mainline.'

Thoughtfully Ralph checked the details. Three were too young, kids who didn't know better, still possible to save. As legal minors they would be sent for hospitalization and shock treatment. Two others were intractable, dropouts in every sense of the word, courting suicide by their misuse of drugs. They would each serve three years in Dexter Prison. The final two were possible.

Chicken-leg Harry was an Afro-American,

the same as Lieutenant Merrow. They made an obvious match. He took Malex Jones.

He watched as a guard ushered the man into the interrogation cubicle. His hair seemed a little too dark for his racial characteristics, his face a little too deeply lined for the age he professed. Ralph waited until he sat then leaned forward across the desk.

'I have to tell you that it is your right to refuse to speak to me this interview is outside the normal procedure of arrest. You may smoke if you wish.'

Malex lit a cigarette. 'For a cop you talk funny. You mean I can get up and go if I want?'

'You may leave this room, yes. But I suggest you stay. It might be to your advantage.'

'So I stay.' Malex shrugged. 'Take away the soft words and what have you got? Just the usual cop routine. What's the matter with you, man? It make you feel better to act the pansy?'

Ralph shrugged. 'Take it anyway you want. Now let's get down to business. You were carrying dope when arrested and you've lost three times already. That means you can get up to five years in Dexter.'

'So?'

'Five years is a long time. I suggest you think about it for a while.'

He sat back, studying the shielded dial of the tell-tale. Malex was sweating and inwardly rigid with tension despite his outward facade. He had been denied his habit too long and it was beginning to show. The electronic pickups in his chair read his physical reactions and the message was plain. No man possessed of imagination could have been without fear. Deliberately Ralph played on it, remaining silent until the tension had mounted and the other man was just about to speak.

'The courts aren't gentle with pushers,' he said quietly. 'I know that, under the Act, the user is as guilty as the supplier, but the Judge is human and doesn't like the leeches who batten off the misery of others. He won't be lenient.'

Malex swallowed. 'I wasn't selling'

The needles jumped a little — a lie.

'You were selling,' said Ralph, 'You had to be. How else would you get the money to buy your own supplies?'

'I've got money.'

Another lie.

'Of course you have.' Ralph was ironic. 'And I bet that you can tell us exactly how much, where it is kept and how you got it.' He didn't wait for an answer. 'Now listen. I'm going to give you one last chance to stop playing around and acting tough. You aren't tough. You're a fake. You dye your hair and pretend to be younger than you are in order to mix in with the deadheads. That way you hope to escape notice and gain the protection they always extent to one of their own kind.' Casually he added. 'Who are you working for?'

'I don't know.'

The truth.

'I'll ask you again,' said Ralph tightly. 'And remember this is your last chance to come clean.'

'Jesus, I don't know!' Malex reared in his chair. 'I guess it's the Mafia but how can I be sure? I'm just a pedlar not a top-guy. Hell, man, you gotta believe me!'

The truth.

'All right,' said Ralph. 'I believe you. Now tell me all about it.'

It was the usual story. Malex had done his last term in prison and had come out broke. Inevitably he'd resumed his habit and had grown desperate for money. A prospector had spotted him. A tout had laid it on the line. A supplier had staked him to his first stock of narcotic.

'I don't know who he is,' insisted Malex. 'I pass over the cash and get more supplies.

'How do you make the exchange?'

'I leave the cash and later get the stuff. Sometimes the routing is changed, we make the swap on a cab, or use a locker somewhere. With the bundle they tell me what I owe. I get it or else.'

'And now you get it,' said Ralph. 'Five years and we'll break your habit for free. Unless — ' He broke off, waiting.

Malex ran his tongue over his lower lip. 'A deal?'

'Are you willing to play along?'

'I don't know.' Malex's hands were shaking as he lit another cigarette.

'Suppose you lay it on the line?'

'It's simple. I want as much information as you can get about the suppliers. Get me names, addresses, everything you can and the higher you go the better.'

'A stoolie!' Malex shook his head. 'Hell, man, do you know what you're asking? Those boys play rough. If they suspected me I wouldn't last an hour.'

His fear was genuine but it was the fear of what could happen and not the fear of what was to come. Ralph watched the inward struggle knowing that he had gauged the man correctly and that he would agree.

Coldly he emphasized the alternative. 'Five years in Dexter against the chance to walk out of here a free man. You'll get back all your stuff and, if you get anything, you'll get paid.'

'With a blowtorch.' Said Malex bitterly. 'With a dose of acid in the eyes. With both arms broken at the elbows.'

'Not if you're smart,' said Ralph. 'Well?'

'Have I any choice?'

'You've got a choice. You can waste five

years of your life if that is what you prefer. No liquor, no women, nothing to smoke, nothing decent to eat. You've been in Dexter. You know what to expect.'

'Hell, said Malex. He drew a shuddering breath. 'All right, I'm your boy.'

The truth — for what it was worth. He could renege as soon as he left the building but it was worth the chance. The alternative was to keep him for five years at the taxpayer's expense.

Quietly Ralph said, 'Just in case you're thinking that you can forget the whole thing once you're outside, remember this. You owe us five years. Fall down on the job and, the next time we gather you in, you'll get double. And we'll get you, make no mistake about that. One way or the other we'll get you. Understand?'

'You don't have to spell it out,' said Malex irritably. 'You cops play rough. A rumour spread through the network and I'd be dead.' He crushed out his cigarette. 'Is that all?'

Ralph hesitated then made his decision. 'There's one more thing. I want you to pass the word that you've a customer for some very special stuff. A rich person with a yen to dream. They'll know what you mean. If you get it contact me immediately and I'll take care of the rest.'

Malex narrowed his eyes. 'I'll get protection?'

'That's right. You're one of us now. An undercover agent for UNLEA. Now get out of here and start working.'

Alone he wondered what Hilda would think about their method of recruiting personnel. Not much, he imagined, and even less if she grasped the full implications. It wasn't just a matter of fighting fire with fire. It was the deliberate use of expendables. Malex might come up with useful information or he might end up dead in a gutter. If so it didn't matter. There would always be others to take his place. In war casualties could not be avoided.

At noon he went looking for Colonel Pryor, finding him in the big operations room, staring at the big world-map with its coloured lights and flashing signals. He was a big man, running to fat but still active, a straggle of thin, white hair on his balding skull.

'Order another helicopter sweep over Cambodia,' he snapped to his sides. 'Use the new defoliants on all suspect areas. Check our contacts in Macao as to the rumours regarding the opium trade. Alert customs for full investigation of all passengers and transport arriving from Hong Kong.'

He glanced to where Ralph stood at the edge of the assembly. 'I won't keep you long, Major.'

Ralph nodded and moved away. Casually he studied the maps showing the suspected routes of the narcotic smugglers, the isolated areas in which the white poppies were grown, the secret factories where the crude stuff was processed into morphine and heroin. In South America the Coco-leaf bearing plants were the objects of high security and all unregistered growths ruthlessly destroyed. As were the papayer somniferum and all forms of cannabis indica, the sources of opium and marihuana.

But the world was big and poppies and hemp could be grown almost anywhere. In isolated fields, secret gardens, among other, disguising crops, in buried hydroponic tanks, even in window boxes. To destroy every plant and seed was impossible yet the effort had to be made. An addict without his drug ceased to be an addict. Eliminate the supply and the demand would be frustrated at birth.

And yet no one cared about the rolling fields of tobacco.

'Sorry to have delayed you, Major.' Colonel Pryor came towards Ralph as the last of his aides scurried about their business. 'We had a little flap from the Orient. Those farmers out there cannot be convinced that they should not grow prescribed plants. You can't wholly blame them, I suppose, they're easy crops and bring a high return. But unless they toe the line we'll have to irradiate the soil with radioactive.'

He meant it. To the colonel it was a serious thing.

He led the way into his office, sat, and gestured to a chair. 'Sit down, Major. I've read your report on the Howarth woman. Have you anything further to add?'

'Not as yet, sir. I'm waiting for the

run-through I ordered from the computer.'

'I have it here.' Pryor picked up a sheaf of papers and tossed them across the desk. 'I also had a complaint from the programmers that you were a little too pressing with your demands.'

'I asked them to hurry. If that is pressing then I apologise.'

'Don't. I told them that battles weren't won by taking coffee breaks and that when one of my officers says 'fast' that is exactly what he means.' Pryor cracked his face into a bleak smile. 'They didn't like it but they had to take it. Military rank and discipline has its advantages.' He grew serious. 'You are quite positive as to the Howarth woman?'

'Yes, sir. Unfortunately I am.'

Pryor shock his head. 'A bad business, Major. A woman like that. Rich, influential, with everything she needs. Why the devil did she do it?'

Ralph shrugged. 'If we knew the answer to that, Colonel, we could solve our problem. Why do any of them do it? For kicks? For escape? From boredom? I read somewhere that the deliberate misuse of drugs is a toying with the death-wish. That, in a sense, it is symbolic suicide. How else to explain the conscious urge to poison the system?'

'I don't know,' Pryor said. 'They do it, that's all we're concerned with, and we have to stop them. But to return to the Howarth woman. Are you sure that it is what you claim?'

'It has to be, sir. She is rich and would have little trouble obtaining the usual narcotic. Her psychological profile shows that she is strong-willed and would never willingly become an addict. She was absolutely desperate or she would never have appealed to me. That means that her original source of supply has dried up which is inconceivable as regards the usual run of narcotics.'

'The supplier could have been holding up the supply in order to inflate the price,' suggested Pryor shrewdly.

'It's barely possible,' admitted Ralph, 'but I doubt it. Through her he had access to the Pent Crowd and that would have been worth more to him than a vicious kill. No, as I see it the supply has dried up. That gives us a lead.'

'Hence your demand for the run-through.' Pryor nodded. 'Well, Major, I hope you find something. You're going to have to work damned hard to do it.'

It was work Ralph was good at. Taking the papers back to his office he settled down to study them. The drug he suspected Cybele of having used was manufactured only by one Drug Company and then only in small, carefully regulated amounts. Like Pryor he was firmly convinced that it should not be manufactured at all but the present state of legislation made it impossible to totally prescribe it. Research chemists demanded their tools regardless of their potential dangers.

It was barely possible that there was a connection between someone having access to the drug and Cybele.

The run-through listed the total of those working for the company in order of access both actual and probable. It listed the sum total of their close contacts and casual acquaintances in similar order.

It also listed Cybele's friends, contacts, associates and relatives. The names ran into the thousands. Without the aid of the computer it would have been impossible to make any correlations within a useful period. Even so, with the groundwork done, it was going to be a dong job.

Ralph ordered coffee and removed his jacket.

There was no direct contact, of course, that would have been hoping for too much. Someone with access might have known someone who knew someone else who knew her. The permutations could become astronomical and so had been kept down to three active parties. The prime, the in-between, the target.

He was sure only of the target, Cybele.

Her face swam before him as he concentrated on the closely typed papers, the diagrams and schematics, the compressed, computer symbolism. Pale in the comet-light, the eyes dark wells of haunting despair, the tears like pearls against her cheeks. She had been like an animal, hurt, afraid, stubborn in her refusal to admit the obvious.

He leaned back, closing his eyes in order to better recall the scene. At first he had been gentle and then, later, he had tried pressure. He had even offered immunity for her cooperation. But he hadn't threatened and was glad of it. Not because it would have been useless but because he was a man and she was a women and, with her, brutality had no place.

He opened his eyes as the phone rang. It was the information room. 'Major Mancini?'

'Yes?'

'Report of the movement of Mrs. Howarth.' The girl's face was expressionless in the screen. 'Information forwarded as requested. The lady in question left for Africa an hour ago. Flight 739 landing at Lagos, Nigeria.'

'Thank you,' said Ralph.

The animal running, he thought as the connection was broken. It fitted the classical pattern. Too many people retained the concept that foreign countries were rich with opportunities to obtain prescribed material. She would stay at the best hotel and drop loaded hints to those who catered to the whims of the rich and spoiled. She would meet touts and gents and those willing to please but unable to supply. Almost he wished that she might be lucky for then the watching UNLEA men would gain a lead.

But they wouldn't, M.D.M wasn't to be gained on an African Shopping expedition.

M.D.M Molybomaine-dextrazide-mecalizine. The latest curse from the pharmaceutical world, non-toxic, non-addictive. Physically harmless.

Psychological hell.

9

Jack Kelman drew a deep breath, held it, released it slowly from his lungs. The breath of Freedom, he thought. The wine of liberty. Is this what it's supposed to be like?

He tried again, feeling the acridity of chemical pollution tear at his chest. The stink of fuming exhausts, of garbage, of sweat and body-odour, of dirt and dust and decay. The air in Dexter had never been like this. The air in there had been sterilized, washed, cleaned, delivered at a controlled temperature. After three years natural air stank raw to his nostrils and scratched at his lungs.

He coughed and spat mucus. He would acclimatize, he knew, but it would take a little time. First he had to find somewhere to live and adapt to the new routine. He had to get outside some decent food and build up his strength. He had some money and the clothes in which he'd been arrested. It was enough. He'd been born with less.

'Hi, mister!' She was one of the harpies always to be found outside any prison. No longer young and far from beautiful but attractive enough to men who hadn't seems a living female in years. Her skirt was short and tight around buttocks and thighs. Her breasts thrust with artificial prominence against the thin material of her blouse. Cosmetics masked her face but nothing could mask the shrewd hard, merciless eyes. Her lips twisted in the simulacrum of a smile. 'Done long?'

'Three years.'

She whistled. 'Man, that's a hell of a long time to be locked in a coop. You got money?'

He nodded.

'Somewhere to stay?'

'Not yet.'

'Then how about staying with me? I've got a little place not too far from here. It's small but real cosy.'

She stepped closer and rested her hand on the sleeve of his jacket so as to feel the material. It looked expensive but it didn't hurt to make sure. 'It's just right for two. A nice, soft, double bed. Steaks in the freezer and a bottle on ice. I owe a little rent but if you can take care of it you're welcome to stay as long as you like. It's got everything.'

Including rats, bugs, venereal disease and a pimp lurking close to take his money and to beat him up if he objected.

'No thanks,' he said.

'Why not?' Her hand tightened on his arm. 'I like you and I bet you could give me quite a time. Three years means a lot of energy locked up and raring to go. Let's go and do something about it.'

'It's still no.' He shook free his arm. 'Now forget it.'

Her face tightened with anger. 'What's the matter? You too good for me? Or maybe you prefer men?'

'You stinking tramp,' he said. 'I wouldn't go with you for pay. Now beat it while you can still walk.'

Twenty yards down the road he caught a cab. The driver grinned as he climbed into the rear compartment.

'I saw you with Suzie. That hustler

never gives up. You want I should take you to where there's something decent?'

'No.'

'Where then?'

'A hotel. Not too pricey and somewhere close to a gymnasium.'

The driver blinked, then smiled. 'I get it but, man, you're way out of touch. The gyms are dead now. The saunas are the places for you gay guys. I know a nice little hot-spot with its own baths and plenty of custom.'

'Just take me where I told you,' said Kelman flatly. 'And keep the clock low — I'm no tourist.'

The cabbie took him to a modest hotel in a run-down street crouched in the shadow of a fly-over. The price was reasonable and he booked a room. It contained a narrow bed, a chair, a cracked washbasin and a flyspecked mirror. The carpet was a faded rag and the walls needed a coat of paint. The wardrobe and bureau were split and a child could have picked the lock but the place had a window and he was alone.

Relaxing on the bed he stared out of

the window. He could see the facade of the buildings opposite, the sweep of the flyover and a few square inches of sky. From the overhead road came the continuous drone of speeding vehicles the walls vibrating a little in sympathy with their passage. An advertising sign on the building opposite, faded in the daylight, flashed a red invitation to drink JAMAICA RUM. Another, in green, said CHILI.

He tensed as footsteps echoed from the passage outside. He heard the murmur of voices and the closing of a door followed by the creak of bedsprings hard at work. The sound disturbed him and he rose and went downstairs. The clerk was a withered owl sitting on the perch of his stool. He looked up form a newspaper as Kelman approached.

'You want something, mister?'

'Where can I eat around here?'

'There's Mexican food across the street, Chinese on the corner, Indian fifty yards down and macrobiotic two blocks away.'

'To hell with that stuff,' said Kelman. 'Where can I get a steak?'

'Turn right, go one block, turn left and the Steakery is two blocks down.'

'And the gym?'

'A block past the Steakery.' The clerk looked at him with fresh interest. 'Are you a fighting man?'

'No,' said Kelman. 'Not yet.'

He ate a light meal of steak and salad going light on the coffee and avoiding the bread. The steak was coarse and loaded with tendering salt but it was meat and he stuffed it down. He walked for an hour to let it settle then headed for the gym.

Like the rest of the area it had seen better days. A big hall filled with a couple of rings, punch bags, ropes and bars. A smaller room held lockers and there were a couple of showers and an old man who claimed to be a masseur. He nodded to where a crowd huddled around one of the rings.

'You're lucky. We've got the champion in here today.'

Kelman caught a glimpse of gleaming ebony skin and a close-cropped head. 'A boxer?'

'Nah, Sutton's the best with a knife

there is! He works the privates but he comes in here sometimes to get a workout. You fancy your chance I could fix you up. Practice knives and it'll only cost you twenty more than you pay for entry.'

Twenty dollars extra for the chance to collect a few shallow gashes and the boast that he'd fought the champion.

'No thanks,' said Kelman.

'Suit yourself.' The old man shrugged. 'That'll be five for the entry and help yourself to a locker. Stay as long as you like. Showers are free but if you want me to rub you down it'll cost another five.'

Stripped to his shorts Kelman began to get himself back into shape. He was soft, flabby, unused muscles weak and aching with protest as he sweated over the equipment. A thief didn't really need muscle but he did need agility and it helped if he could beat off any opposition. Kelman had to get back into condition before he could go into business.

He heard a yell from the crowd as he paused, chest heaving from his exertions.

'Did you see that!' A man turned, face

red with excitement. 'Right down the ribs and three times across in a triple-slash! Man, is he fast!'

'He's fast.' Agreed his companion. 'Neilson might have taken him two years ago but Sutton's the best there is now.'

'Neilson was never that good. He showed it when Ingati took him in a hundred and eighty-four. Sutton took Ingati in the preliminary and didn't even sweat.'

He craned his neck as he tried to see into the ring. 'Well, that's it for today. He's run out of partners.'

Kelman retreated as the crowd broke up. A cluster of sycophants hung around the fighter as he headed for the private door. No one took any notice of the dozen young men who sat, nursing their wounds, trying to smile above their pain.

'All right, lads.' The old man was eager for business. 'I've got salve and dressings in the office. Five each and I'll fix you up better than any doctor. And you'll have scars to show for it,' he added temptingly. 'Something to show your girl. Proof that you've been up against the champ.'

Kelman returned to his exercises as they filed into the office. He worked until he ached, knowing that he would suffer from sore muscles but willing to accept the discomfort for the sake of speed. He had money enough to last maybe ten days. At the end of that time he had to be ready.

It was getting late when, showered and rested, he finally left the gym. He walked for a while and then had another meal in a better class place than the Steakery. He had a tenderloin with eggs and a helping of liver, salad, but no bread or potatoes. From the restaurant he went to a movie and watched twenty-year old films until it was almost midnight.

The girl was a shadow in a doorway as he neared his hotel.

'Hello, there!'

He paused, eyes searching the street for a sign of anyone lurking close, then looked at the girl as she approached. She was young, quietly dressed, in direct contrast to the harpy who had propositioned him outside the prison. Her face was pale and her eyes held a peculiar glitter. Kelman had seen that glitter before and he relaxed. She was a junkie after earning the price of a fix.

'How about it,' she said quietly. 'You look as if you could use what I've got to offer.'

That and more. Much more. He could use what the whole world had to offer.

Why not begin with the girl?

'My place?'

'But of course.' She linked her arm in his, smiling, no longer tense now that she had solved her immediate problem. 'Is it far?'

Inside the room he drew the curtains and cut down the light room outside, muting the flaring red and green into a subdued combination of colour that blackened their lips but did nothing to alter the texture of her skin. Stripped she lay on the bed, watching as he shed his clothes. She had already been paid — the rest was a matter of simple execution. The sooner he finished the sooner she would be on her way.

He couldn't make it.

He tried, sweating with the desperate

need to prove himself.

The girl looked at him, her eyes shadows against the oval of her face. 'What's the matter? Is something wrong?'

'Not with you.'

He tensed, expecting laughter or a sneering insult and had she given it he would have killed her where she lay. But she was older than she seemed.

'Don't worry about it,' she said quietly. 'It can happen to anyone. Why don't you take a little something to cure it?'

'Such as?'

'I don't know. Something to give you a boost. The stuff must be around if you need it. If you've got a headache you take some aspirin. A stomach ache some bicarbonate. Where is the difference? You know,' she said, 'I used to work in a drug store once. You'd be surprised at the stuff the factories turn out. Tablets that can lift you right up when you're feeling low. Pills to make you sleep. Powders to kill your worries. You should be able to walk into a shop and buy what you need. You could too,' she ended bitterly, 'if it wasn't for the crummy doctors.'

'You don't like them?'

'You're damn right I don't like them! Little tin gods sitting on their fat rears and telling you what you can't have. What right have they to give the orders? You go to one with a problem and maybe he's religious or moral or has his own goddam notion as to the way you should live. You want something to cure a misery and he turns you down. He lets you suffer when all the time all he's got to do is to make a few squiggles on a paper. We've got enough Big Brothers without having them riding on our backs!'

'So that lets me out,' said Kelman bitterly. 'I go to a quack and tell him what's wrong and he gives me a lecture on morals. To hell with that.'

'You don't have to go to a quack. There are other ways of getting the stuff.'

He reared up on one elbow. 'You could get it for me?'

'If you want me to, sure, but I don't think you need it. You're tired. Overdoing it, maybe. You're trying too hard and letting failure get you down. So what if you can't make it right this minute? You will.' She smiled up at him from the pillow. 'Don't worry about it. I've seen it happen before. Lots of times. There's nothing really the matter with you.'

Perhaps the exercise had taken the stuffing out of him. The excitement of release from prison, the good food, the walking.

'You're just tired,' she insisted. 'Get some sleep and when you wake up you'll be fine. You'll see.'

But when he woke, both she and his money were gone.

10

An ambulance stood next door when Joe arrived home and he stood, watching as attendants carried a sheeted figure to the waiting vehicle. The inevitable crowd pressed close and the inevitable cop yelled the inevitable command.

'Get back there! Get back!'

As if a man didn't have a right to see what was going on.

'A bad business, Mr. Connors.' Solomon Asch was a round, aging man who spent most of his time sitting on the sidewalk, perched on a folding chair and watching the world pass by. 'No one is safe in their own homes now.'

'Who was it?'

'Old Mrs. Farrell. Eighty-seven if a day. The poor soul lived alone and had nothing. They found her lying in a pool of her own blood. Her room was ripped apart and she had been beaten to death.' Asch puffed out his cheeks and shook his head. 'A bad business when that can happen, Mr. Connors. A terrible business.'

Joe grunted as the ambulance pulled away, siren wailing. 'Murdered was she? And what are the police doing?'

'Break it up there!' yelled the cop. 'Keep moving!'

Asch shrugged. 'What can they do? They ask questions and take notes but I doubt if they can do more. I may even have seen those who killed her. A couple of young men with a look about them who left running. But how to be sure? So many pass in and out.'

'Did you tell the police that?'

'No, Mr. Connors. I remained silent. I do not want to have to go and look at endless photographs and have endless interviews. And what could I say? I am an old man and my memory is not what it was. I saw two young men but I could not describe them. They could be innocent and I do not want to get involved.'

A wise policy, thought Joe. The tenements were crowded and it didn't pay to do other than mind your own business.

He remembered gossip he'd heard about the old woman. Without family or friends she'd lived alone in a tiny cubicle and the rumour was that she'd had some items of jewellery tucked away, mementoes of better days. So someone had tried to collect and had hit her a little too hard in order to make her talk.

Mary had a different idea. She turned from the stove as he entered the apartment, hair straggled about her sweating face, figure shapeless beneath her faded robe. 'Heard about the murder?'

'Yes.' Joe shed his coat and hung it on a nail. The kitchen-living room was ten feet by eight. Beyond it lay a bedroom twelve feet by ten which contained two double beds. They shared toilet facilities with three other families and a bathroom with six.

'I figure the Gowers did it,' she said, stirring a pot. 'They never did like the idea of her having a room to herself while they had to share. I know they had the promise of it when she died. They could have helped her along,'

'And fixed it to look like a robbery?' Joe nodded, it made sense, but it was none of their business. 'What's for dinner?'

It was the usual hash, a pap of cereal, vegetables, pasta and a few shreds of processed meat. The leftovers of the day brought to a boil. He spooned it down with mounting distaste then thrust aside the bowl as anger ruined his appetite.

'Why the hell do I have to eat this crap? All the time it's hash, hash, goddam hash! You think I'm a hog or something?'

'Good food costs money,' she said. 'If you want steak get a better job.'

'So you can ride higher on my back?' He glared his rage as he picked up the bowl and returned the contents to the pot. 'Every goddam cent I earn goes in this place and for what? Shared beds and pots of hash, that what. Call this a life?'

'You're whining again, Joe.' Mary turned from the stove, pushing back her hair. 'If you had any guts at all you'd get out and get more instead of complaining all the time. When I married you, you had ambitions. What happened to the gas station we were going to have? The agency? All the plans you used to talk about?'

'Shut up!'

'Why should I?' She glared at him where he sat crammed against the table. 'You think I like living like this?'

'If you don't like it,' he said tightly, 'you know what you can do.'

'Quit?' she shook her head. 'You'd like that, wouldn't you? For us to walk out and leave you alone. Well, Joe, that isn't going to happen. You can leave if you want but you've a wife and children to take care of and the law will see that you do it!'

'Some kids!' he was bitter. 'A damned deadhead for a son and a tart for a daughter. What are you doing about that, anyway? Did you see the welfare?'

'About what?'

'About an abortion, that's what! You think I want to be saddled with the upkeep of a bastard on top of everything else?' He sat, fuming. 'It's all your fault. Had you kept an eye on her this wouldn't have happened. Thirteen years old and knocked up already. For Christ's sake do something about it!'

'I have.' She sat, facing him, face shining from the heat trapped in the tiny room. 'An abortion will cost three thousand dollars paid in advance.'

'What!' He slammed his hand on the table. 'Where the hell am I going to get *that* kind of money? Why can't they do it for less? The government — '

'They won't touch it, Joe. The welfare don't want to know. If it's going to be done at all it has to be done privately.'

'That's a hell of a thing!' He felt his anger rise and threaten to choke him. 'All the time they tell us to cut down the population and when you try to do it what happens? You can't, that's what. Just because some moralistic bastards crack the whip. They don't believe in it or something. Goddam it without dough a man doesn't stand a chance!'

He rose and crossed to the faucet laving his face and neck with cold water. The wash didn't help. Still seething he looked at his wife, still sitting at the table, rough hands clasped on the stained surface.

'Where are they now? The kids I mean.'

'Ginny is with some friends. I don't know where Gerry is.'

Joe flung down the towel. At sixteen his son could be anywhere and the way he felt at the moment if he never saw him again that would be just fine. At least he wouldn't have to share a bed with him when he worked days. Not that it made much difference now if the two kids slept together. The damage had been done.

'What's she feel about it? Ginny I mean.'

Mary said quietly, 'She wants to keep the baby. I think she should.'

'For Christ's sake, why? Who the hell is going to marry her with a kid hanging around? And who the hell is going to support it? Me?'

'It won't be so bad, Joe.' Mary rose and faced him. 'I can maybe get a job to help out and we can cut down a little. You could even get a raise.' Her shoulders were slumped, beaten. 'Anyway, what else can we do?'

'Kick her out, that's what!' He said harshly. 'These goddam kids go their own way when it suits them so to hell with them. She knew what she was doing. To hell with her!'

'You don't mean that, Joe.'

'Like hell I don't!'

'All right,' she said, suddenly angry. 'You just try to kick her out and see what happens. You've got a legal duty to support her and if you don't want to wind up in jail that's just what you're going to do. She's your daughter, remember. As a parent you've got to look after her when she's in trouble.'

He was sarcastic. 'Like your folks did? When you got yourself knocked up with Gerry did they stand by you?'

'I was seventeen, Joe.'

'Sure, a nice little innocent girl who knew a good thing when she saw it. A soldier off overseas with plenty of insurance in case he got himself killed. So you let me have it then turned the screw. Jesus! I must have been crazy to have fallen for that old line!'

Her lips tightened as she blinked away tears. 'I was in love with you, Joe. I thought you were in love with me too.'

'I married you, didn't I? What more did you want?'

A hell of a lot more, he thought, looking at her. We both did. Somewhere nice to live, a normal family, some love and respect and understanding. Not two rooms in a slum with hash five days a week, no decent clothes, kids you could only be ashamed of, a job that provided a uniform and little else.

'To hell with it,' he said. 'I'm going out.'

It was growing dark when he hit the street with a fine drizzle of rain, which gave everything a greasy shine. Habit carried him to Charlie's, a semi-subterranean cellar with a bar, a television screen, a couple of computer game machines and a row of one-armed bandits. A man greeted him as he entered.

'Hi, Joe. Beer?'

'Thanks.' He took the glass and lifted it. 'Here's to health, Scott.'

Together they drank.

'A hell of a night,' said Scott Irwin. He was a big, red-faced man of Joe's own age and they had served together overseas on a peace-keeping mission. Now he drove a cab and hated every minute of it. 'Two bum calls and a smart guy tried to jump out at a set of lights.' His laugh was ugly. 'You should have seen his face when he found I'd locked him in. Damn creeps! They make me sick.'

Joe drank more of his beer. 'What did you do?'

Took him for a forty dollar ride and made him pay for it.'

'No tip?'

'Ten for my trouble. He threatened to call a cop so I pasted him one for luck.' Scott looked at his knuckles. 'He won't call a cop. He was damn lucky I didn't squash his guts under a wheel!'

Joe ordered more beer, envying his friend his toughness. Scott was a hard man to cross. Casually he said, 'How's Shelia?'

'That damned whore!'

Joe waited. She was Scott's wife, a lovely girl half his age with a figure designed to please.

'She's walked out on me,' said Scott bitterly. 'Left me a note saying she'd be sending me the divorce papers.' His big hand closed around his glass. 'If I ever find the bitch I'll kill her!'

'Maybe she'll change her mind.' Said Joe optimistically. 'Come back to you.'

'Nah. She's probably signed on with some call-girl agency. Easy dough for looking at ceilings. The cow! She was peddling it around when I met her but I figured that she was willing to play it straight. Well, I was wrong.' He finished his beer. 'Have another.'

They had five more and Joe stopped worrying about the expense. What the hell, a man had to have a little fun, didn't he? And Scott was an old friend. An old buddy from a better time. It was good to sit and chew the fat for a while.

Joe drank more beer. 'Remember how we pulled that sting on the shopkeepers? Selling them PX. Supplies then going back and taking them off the shelves as stolen items?'

'They couldn't tell us apart,' chuckled Joe. 'We got paid to forget we'd had them.' He stared into his glass. 'Good times, Scott. What the hell happened to them?'

'We came home,' said Scott. 'Me to a stinking cab and a cheating wife. You to a crummy job where you act as a lackey in a monkey-suit. To hell with it. The past is dead.'

Dead but not forgotten. After Scott had left to pick up a fare Joe sat brooding over his beer. He should have stayed in the army, he thought. He'd have made sergeant and maybe stayed overseas. Or he could have become a mercenary. There were always Middle East hotspots. There had been opportunities for a smart man and he could have found himself a place. But there had been Mary and the kid and the lure of home. He should have turned his back on them all and kept running while he had the chance.

Outside the rain had turned into a mist that fogged the lamps and wetted his face. He breathed deeply, still living in the past, remembering the feel of his uniform, the sense of power the pistol at his belt had imparted, the rifle and grenades, the knife and helmet and appurtenances of war. No one had pushed him around in those days. Then he had been respected and had belonged. There had been good comradeship and fun and times of fevered excitement. Why the hell had he ever left the army?

Half-dreaming he began to walk home, keeping by ingrained habit to the centre of the sidewalk. Muggers lurked in doorways and drivers were sometimes careless. The shining red and green and amber, orange and blue and smoking violet, so that he seemed to walk alone in a gleaming fairyland.

It was the beer, he thought, swaying a little. The beer and the talk and good old Scott with his memories of the past. A damn shame about Shelia though. Just as he was beginning to think he was making a little time. Well, just as well she had gone. He could have landed in trouble there and Scott was a tough character. He swayed again and plunged down a shadowed side street.

Halfway down he realised that he was being followed.

There were two of them, dark shapes walking on rubber soles, eyes and teeth flashing. They wore tight trousers, black shirts, leather jackets and hoods. Each carried a tightly rolled newspaper. Harmless newsprint but when so rolled having the near-consistency of wood, able to thrust and strike with devastating effect.

Damn the government for denying a man the means with which to protect himself!

Abruptly sober Joe lengthened his stride. He reached another street and headed down it towards a junction bright with light. Fear rose within him as he heard the accelerating pad of footsteps. They would catch him before he could reach the dubious safety of the light area and if not it made no difference. They would follow him as far as he wished to go and then, when ready, they would strike.

Or perhaps they wouldn't. Perhaps they were just playing a game, riding his back until his nerve broke and he started to run. It was a chance he dared not take.

Ten known murders a day in this city alone — and who bothered to count the muggings?

He halted as the pad of footsteps drew

closer, turning, anger rising to replace his fear.

'All right,' he said flatly. 'What do you want?'

They slowed, coming to a halt six feet away, black faces sullen in the shadow of their hoods. Their rolled newspapers were held like swords. Joe remembered similar incidents in his army days, impassive brown faces with enigmatic eyes, masks for hate and burning anger.

'Come on,' he said, 'I asked you a question. Why are you following me? What do you want?'

'Money,' said one. 'For a cup of coffee.'

'That's right, man,' said his companion.

'All right,' said Joe. He was suddenly calm, his mind cold despite his seething rage, the sudden accelerated pounding of his heart. This is it, he thought. It's you or them. If you've any guts at all now is the time to show it. Damn them! The stinking bastards!

He pulled his wallet from his hip pocket and threw it to the ground.

'Now, man,' said the first one. 'That

ain't polite. That ain't no way to treat strangers who just want to get a cup of coffee on a wet night.'

'That's right,' said his companion. 'Now you just bend down and pick it up and give us the money real gentleman-like.'

Joe stepped forward, stooping as though he intended to pick up the wallet. Before he touched it he straightened, boot lashing out at the groin of the one who stood to his left. He felt the impact, the soggy yielding and heard the sudden shriek of raw agony. He continued the movement, spinning in a circle, dimly remembered scraps of unarmed combat training coming to mind. He reached out as he faced the other man, knocking aside the thrusting paper, clamping his hands over the shadowed face. He felt the eyes beneath his thumbs and pressed viciously against a sudden gush of warm wetness and the horrible scream of pain. Stooping he snatched up his wallet and raced down the street.

Three turnings later he halted and wiped away the blood from his hands and the leather with his handkerchief. Mary did the laundry so he wanted no mark. Wadding it into a ball he threw it aside and, drawing a deep breath, strode boldly towards home.

It had been so easy! So goddam easy!

They depend on fear, he told himself. They're like a snake tracking a rabbit, hypnotising the creature with its own terror and so making it easy prey. Well, he thought, this time they picked on the wrong guy. They picked on a tiger when they thought they faced a pussy. All it needs is the determination to act and to do it fast and hard. Hit first and cripple before they know what's happening. Their own confidence makes them helpless. And to think he'd been scared!

It was all an attitude of mind, he decided. A point of view. You could be a sheep or a wolf and the difference was in the way you looked at things. Thugs picked on their victim following the rules. Obey the law and you were sunk because they didn't obey it and so had all the advantage. They didn't expect you to kick them in the groin or to gouge out their eyes because law-abiding people didn't do things like that. Law-abiding people depended on the police to give them protection and where were the police when needed?

Where had they been tonight?

Goddam it, in this world a man had to be ready to defend himself no matter what the government might say!

11

He was an old man dressed in a soiled shirt and slacks, canvas shoes on his bare feet and a loose scarf wrung around his throat. The shirt was stained over the region of the heart with an oozing patch of blood. His hands were limp the knuckles prominent and the backs flecked with the brown patches of age. One palm held a blackened puncture. He had no head.

'The neurological boys took it,' explained Inspector Frere, looking at the plastic seal covering the stump of the severed neck. 'They left a while before you arrived. I've got a photo if you want to see what he looked like.'

Ralph studied the coloured image. The face was relaxed in death, the blue eyes prominent and traced with a mesh of thin red lines. The nose was a hooked beak and the mouth had once been cruel.

'Whoever hit him came close,' said

Frere. He had the sombre eyes and drooping mouth of a Dalmatian and if he resented the presence of the UNLEA man he managed to hide it. 'He threw up his hand to stop the bullet. A reactive gesture, I guess and the change left powder marks all over his palm.'

Ralph frowned. 'If so close why shoot at all? He was an old man and his skull must have been pretty thin. A swing of the barrel would have taken care of him without making a lot of noise. Why take a chance that someone would investigate the shot?'

'Now you're thinking like a cop,' Frere said. 'This thing was done by a scared kid most like. A professional would have figured it the same as you but then a professional wouldn't have used a gun in the first place. Guns,' he said bitterly. 'We do our best but they keep coming to light. Once a kid gets one in his hand he thinks he has the world by the tail.'

Ralph made no comment. The world in which they lived was one the adults had made and the heritage of violence stemmed from the dawn of time.

'Damn kids,' Frere muttered. 'They want it all on a silver plate and they want it yesterday. When they get it they throw it right back in your face.' He looked at Ralph. 'Have you got any kids?'

'No.'

'You could be lucky. They're nice when they're small but they don't stay that way. They get big and start elbowing for room. At times I wonder if we're breeding true. You know? Mutations and all that. Kids now don't seem to be the same as they did. No respect. No patience. Nothing.'

His voice was bitter with introspection and Ralph guessed that he had a private grief. He drew attention back to the corpse.

'You're sure about who did this? That it was a kid, I mean.'

'I'm sure.' Frere stepped back as a finish-up photographer got to work with his camera. 'Some youngster who some-how managed to get hold of a gun and tried a stick-up on the strength of it. Maybe the old guy wouldn't scare or maybe he scared too fast and went too far. He could have got panic-stricken,' he explained. 'Tried to jump the kid as a last-chance effort. Well, it was his last chance right enough.' He blinked as the photographer flashed for his holograms.

Ralph looked thoughtfully at the Inspector, unsatisfied with his facile summation. 'Why did they do it? What did they hope to gain?'

'They?'

'The ones who did this.'

'Kids.' To Frere that was explanation enough. 'Who knows what they wanted? Whoever knows? Some easy money, perhaps. A kick out of scaring the enemy. That's us,' he said grimly. 'To any kid any adult is the enemy. Or perhaps it was an initiation. You know the sort of thing, kill someone before joining the gang. Who knows?'

And who cares, thought Ralph. Really cares. Not you who represent the police who are supposed to protect the life and property of the citizen, But that was being unfair. The police did what they could but there was too much to do and not enough men to do it. Crowd control, riot control, traffic and queue control. Patrols and calls and constant duty and, always, the sullen antagonism of those they were employed to serve.

Leaving the body Ralph looked around. The dead man had owned a small store with newspapers, magazines, candy, tobacco, stationery, soft drinks and ice cream as his items of trade. A place that must have taken eighteen hours a day to operate with a minimal return. He watched as the inspector checked the register. The drawer made a sharp ringing sound as it opened.

'Anything left?'

'A few bills and some change but he wouldn't have kept much in the register anyway.' Frere slammed shut the drawer. 'It looks as if nothing was taken. I guess whoever shot him ran off without waiting around to help himself.'

'So he wasn't robbed,' said Ralph. 'At least as far as we know. How long was it before you found the body?'

'Not long. A woman heard the shot and looked inside. She called us when she saw the dead man. I reported it under standard procedure and the next thing I know the neurological boys are after his head. Then you arrive. It seems a lot of trouble to be taking over a routine shooting.'

It was the expected resentment finally beginning to show. Ralph had expected it, the natural irritation of an overworked officer at the weight of high and over-riding pressure.

'You know how these things work, Inspector. All reported crimes are fed into the computer. If anything comes up of interest to UNLEA someone like me is sent down to find out what we can. That is why the head was taken and why I am here. I'm sure that I can enjoy your full cooperation and that we can work on this together.'

Frere looked mollified. 'He was something special?'

'That's right,' said Ralph. 'And that's the reason I don't want to rush this.' He wandered around this store casually examining items selected at random. The magazines were the inevitable pornography. The candy was dusty in its wrappers and the toys soiled with neglect and time. Only the newspapers were fresh. 'The dead man's real name is Jorge Olsen. He was a qualified chemist who once tried to make a fortune by the illegal manufacture of lysergic acid diethylamide, LSD. It's easy enough if you know how and he had the knowledge. That attempt cost him ten years in jail. He got out two years ago.'

'So?'

'This store needn't be all it seems. And he was murdered but not, as far as we know, robbed. It could be as you suspect, a senseless killing by some stupid youngster, or it could be something more than that. It's just possible that this thing could lead to something else.'

'Narcotics?' The inspector was interested and alert to the obvious implications. 'You think that maybe he'd gone back into business and was making the stuff and using this store as a front to sell it?'

'Perhaps. That's why I want to look around.'

'Could I help?'

Ralph doubted it, the inspector lacked the specialised training to be of use, but he didn't say so. Instead he said, 'I'd appreciate your help. Look around and, if you see anything which doesn't quite appear what it should be, let me know.'

Ralph continued his inspection. A back room opened on the rear of the store, a living room by its appearance containing a personal computer and high-priced television and stereophonic system. A cocktail cabinet held an assortment of cut glass and bottles of imported liquor. Two other rooms were respectively a kitchen and a bedroom. The freezer in the bathroom was off the bedroom, which held an oversized bed fitted with inflatable cushions and a carpet of ankle deep wool. A projector built into the headboard of the bed sprang into life as he pressed a control. On a wall couples writhed in pagan abandon. Ralph switched off the instrument and, frowning, returned to the store.

'Find anything?' Frere turned from where he was busy probing through the stock.

'Not yet,' said Ralph.

He examined the shelves and selected certain items. The inspector followed him into the kitchen where he selected more.

On the extra-large kitchen table Ralph began to assemble a complex apparatus from storage jars, lengths of plastic tubing, a hotplate, an electrically powered eggbeater, some covered bowls, slim tubes of plastic from a display and several other items.

The inspector was intrigued. 'What are you doing?'

'Just testing a theory.' Ralph prowled through the kitchen acutely aware of the inspector's watching eyes. 'I'm looking for a length of twisted glass or plastic tubing,' he said. 'Have you any idea where one might be kept?'

'In this thing,' said Frere, pointing to a long, narrow box fitted over the sink. 'It's a pure-water distilling apparatus. You remember they were all the rage five years back when we had that big typhoid scare. People don't use then so much now aside from those who like to make their own hooch.'

Ralph nodded, opened the box and slipped out the coil of glass. He fitted it into his apparatus and then made a series of adjustments. Finally he took a variety of fluids from the cabinet, tasted them, diluted some with water from the faucet and fed them into the assembled mass of glass and plastic. They were of different colours and consistencies.

'Now what?' said Frere.

'We wait.' Ralph led the way into the living room. 'And while we're waiting look around.'

The place held few hiding places and no secret panels. As Ralph checked the undersides of the furniture and probed into the p.c. and television set the inspector checked through a row of books.

'Is this something?' He held up a sheet of paper. 'It looks like equations of some kind. Can you make any sense out of it?'

Ralph took the paper. It was handwritten and covered with an intricate chemical formula. His face hardened as he realised what he held. 'Is there anything else?'

'Only an envelope addressed to the Society for the Preservation of Individual Liberties.' Frere looked blank. 'That's the SPIL crowd. Why should he be writing to them?'

'Simple. If you wanted to hide a tree where would you put it?'

'In a forest,' said the inspector promptly. 'But what has that got to do with it?'

'Everything,' said Ralph. 'When I first joined the force we had a very interesting case. Suddenly a lot of people received a thousand dollars through the post. The money was in various bills and no two had the same number. With it came a letter with an impressive heading stating that the recipient had been chosen to partake in a specialised market research programme. The money was a gift on two conditions; they would tell no one about it and they would keep a record of how it was spent and what it had meant in terms of increased happiness. The money was counterfeit, of course. Someone had supplicated a thousand genuine dollars on a photo-offset machine.'

Frere looked his puzzlement. 'So? What was the point? If someone wanted to pull a thing like that surely he would keep it to himself. Why be such a fool as to pass it around?'

'He was no fool. We caught three

hundred and seventy people trying to pass those bills and each and every one of them had a perfect alibi. We never did find out how many managed to get away with it but one thing we could be certain of — one of them, or even one of those we caught, was the guilty party.'

'The tree in the forest,' said Frere. 'I get what you mean. Spread a thing around and who can tell from where it first originated? You know, that man was smart. You never caught him, of course?'

'No. He was clever enough not to pull the same thing again in the same area.' Ralph folded the paper and put it together with the envelope into a pocket. 'Let's go and see if what I suspect is correct.'

Back in the kitchen he examined his equipment. The coloured fluids had moved through the apparatus and, by their movement, had told him all he needed to know.

'I want a twenty-four hour a day watch kept on this place' he ordered. 'A secret surveillance. Have scanners put in every room and then remove all personnel.'

'Are you hoping the murderer will return?'

'More than that.' Ralph began dismantling the apparatus, smashing each part as he freed it from the whole. 'Olsen reverted to type,' he explained. 'He couldn't resist the temptation to make an easy fortune. This is a distilling and fractionating plant. It may look a mess but it is really quite efficient. The hot plate has a thermostatic control. The plastic is tested inert. The glassware is fireproof. If you know what you are doing you can take some easily obtainable compounds and from them produce something really nasty.'

'And valuable.' Frere was quick to grasp the implications. 'That's where the money came from to buy that expensive furniture and liquor. You're hoping his contacts will come back as to be spotted.'

'That's right.' Ralph spilled fluids down the sink. 'But Olsen wouldn't have been such a fool as to spend money he couldn't account for. Those expensive items are probably the result of some lucky bets he made or a prize won in a lottery. It isn't hard to buy winning tickets if you're pre-pared to pay over the odds in untaxable cash. That could mean he hasn't been in production for very long. Just long enough to make a sample batch, perhaps, and to line up his outlets.'

'He was an old man,' said Frere thoughtfully. 'It would have been hard for him to deny himself a few luxuries if he had the cash.' He looked at Ralph. 'Was it LSD?'

'Not this time. Olsen had grown ambitious or maybe he wanted to try his skill. This time he was making something much worse.' He flung the last of the dismantled equipment into the sink where it landed with a crash of breaking glass. 'He was making molyboamine dextriaz Mecalizine. MDM.'

'I've heard of it,' said Frere. 'They call it Heaven.'

'That's right,' said Ralph grimly. 'Another name for hell.'

12

On the stage ghosts were singing, the resurrected actors who had died earlier in the play, now on their feet and joining together in a Greek-type chorus which emphasized morality, justice, the intrinsic decency of democratic process and the aspiration of a better world to come.

Ralph looked at Lavinia as the curtain came down. 'What did you think of it?'

'As a play it was pretty awful,' she said. 'The song at the end was even worse.'

'That's just what I thought.' He rose, joining the crowd of first-nighters streaming towards the exits. 'Let's get ourselves a drink to wash away the taste.'

The theatre bar was crowded and it took a while to fill his order. Turning with the drinks in his hand he bumped into someone and recognised John Rigby. The recognition was mutual.

'Major Mencini!' The drama critic held out his hand, dropping it as he saw that both of Ralph's were occupied. 'This is a pleasant surprise. Are you a devotee of the arts?'

'I like to see a play sometimes,' said Ralph dryly.

'Of course, and you must forgive my apparent surprise. It's just that one doesn't usually associate a policeman with cultural pursuits. Not that this shambles can be called that.' Rigby pursed his lips. 'I give it three performances at the most. You agree?'

'Three is being generous,' said Ralph. 'One has been one too many.'

'Then we see eye to eye. Are you alone? No? Then I'll tell you what. Why don't you bring your friend backstage? We are having the usual wake and tonight I feel like drawing blood. Is that your friend?' He waved at Lavinia. 'Do come. We are going to need a little beauty to enliven the proceedings.'

Ralph hesitated. He had intended spending the evening alone with Lavinia but Rigby was a suspect and the chance to get to know the man on an informal footing was too good to miss.

'We'd love to join you,' he said and added, casually, 'Have you seen anything of Cybele lately?'

'Not since the party. I think she's gone abroad somewhere but I don't really know.' Rigby turned as a pale-faced young man with a ruffled shirt and a ring in his ear plucked at his sleeve. 'All right, Derek. You go ahead. I'll join you later.'

'You're sure, John?' The young man was anxious despite his air of bravado, 'I mean, I'd like to hear your views and there are others who will miss you.'

'I'll be along.' Rigby shook his head as the young man moved reluctantly away. 'The author,' he said. 'Derek Burdon. Most of the backing came from his devoted parents and he's hoping to bribe me into giving him a good review. Is he in for a shock. Coming?'

A dozen people occupied the green room together with waiters serving champagne to the producer, director, a couple of angels and a scatter of hopeful actors. A hum of sycophantic conversation filled the air, empty chatter designed to please, rising above the clink of glasses like the murmur of bees.

'A simply marvellous play, darling!' An aging actress gushed over the author. 'I'm really quite consumed with envy. Unless you write me a part in your next production I'll refuse ever to talk to you again.'

'Such depth,' said another, unwilling to be outdone. 'Such sensitivity of feeling. Such boldness in probing to the festering heart of moral and social problems. What do you think, John? Surely you must agree!'

Rigby smiled at Lavinia over the edge of his glass.

'Well now,' he said. 'Tonight we have a unique opportunity to discover what the paying audience thinks of the production. Tell us, my dear, what did you think of the play?'

'I didn't like it!'

The aging actress was quick off the mark. 'Darling, how can you say that? You must be joking! It was a wonderful play!' Her eyes grew shrewd. 'You are qualified to judge, of course? I mean, are you a member of the profession?'

Lavinia smiled. 'Yes. I think you can say that.'

Burdon thrust himself forward, face in a scowl. Against a woman and one without known influence he could afford to be aggressive. 'Why not?' he demanded. 'Just what didn't you like about it?'

'It was hopelessly illogical,' said Lavinia quietly. 'The situations you proposed simply couldn't exist.'

'Illogical? My God!' Burdon threw his hands into the air. 'You fool! Couldn't you see that the action was symbolic? An allegorical statement of existing frameworks of social reference played against a shifting montage of individual viewpoints? And you call it illogical? Heaven save us from the condemnation of fools!'

'I didn't like it either,' said Ralph tightly. 'Do you intend to insult everyone who disagrees with your contention that the play is a masterpiece?'

'You too?' Burdon was acting the part of the artistic author outraged by the Philistines. 'My God! John! What vipers have you brought among us?'

Rigby shrugged. 'They are paying

customer, Derek, and I'd advise you to restrain your rhetoric. My friend is a man of very short temper.' He took a fresh glass of champagne from a passing waiter. 'And before we get all heated perhaps you would like to know what I thought of the production?'

'Of course, John. You, at least are able to appreciate the artistic endeavour and to give a balanced judgement.'

'Thank you, Derek.' Rigby poised his glass and took a sip of the contents. 'This is good champagne,' he said. 'Unfortunately I can't say the same about your play.'

'John — '

'If you'll listen I'll tell you why,' said Rigby, ignoring the interruption. 'I'm not complaining about the acting or the sets or the lighting. They were up to standard. Not wonderful because an actor can only be as good as his dialogue and the lines they had to speak were farcical. The plot was even worse. As Lavinia said, it was so illogical as to be ridiculous, and before you start spouting pretty phrases at me about symbolism and allegories, let me make one thing plain. You are in business and your business is to entertain people. If you offer them something they can't understand they are not entertained and will not pay to see what you offer. That means you go out of business and your artistry, no matter how good you may consider it to be, is lost. In such a case you are to blame because you have failed to communicate. It isn't the job of those who pay to figure out your meaning — it is yours to make sure they can grasp what you're getting at.'

He took another sip of champagne.

'That's the first point. Now let's look at the second. People aren't as foolish as you take them to be. When confronted with something that outrages their intelligence they will react against it. To treat an audience as if they were mental halfwits is one sure way to get a short run. To blast them with pseudo-artistry is another. This play is a combination of both and if you manage to fill the house three nights running it will be a miracle.'

'All right,' said the author. He looked older, the young-rebel facade dissolved beneath the critic's blast which, when published as he knew it would be, could effectively ruin his hopes of a successful hit. 'You don't like the play but you still haven't said why. Not in detail. How was it so illogical — as if that matters?'

'It matters,' said Rigby emphatically. 'And I'll tell you why. A critic has to judge a work in the frame of the references in which it is offered. By that I mean you can't judge one thing in relation to another of a totally different kind. Ibsen is not the same as Dickens. Shaw mustn't be compared to Chekov. A tragedy is not in the same category as a farce. You must weigh the worth of a book or a play within the context of what the author intended. He may chose any rules or relationships he likes but within those rules he must remain logical to his own premises. That is what Lavinia meant when she said your play was hopeless in its logic. The result in those who came to see it, was a mounting sense of outrage and irritation. You had cheated and no one likes that. They don't like to be fooled. Not when they have to spend money for the experience.'

'I'm still waiting,' said Burdon savagely. 'Just how was I illogical?'

'You proposed a rigorous totalitarian system of absolute government which controlled the acts and thinking of the populace — yet you had that same populace all around armed to the teeth. You had two time travellers enter that society from a period that would be the equivalent to that of the Middle Ages compared to our own. These two fall in love with their opposite numbers high in the government. They are prevented from mating by the law. They then are contacted by the underground and, because of the knowledge they bring to the movement, promptly trigger off a successful revolution. Logical? A child would know better.'

'I'm no child,' said Burdon.

'You want it spelled out? First your society would not and could not exist. No totalitarian government would ever allow its populace to walk around fully armed. Second, even allowing for the fact that your characters fell in love and wanted to mate, what's so special about marriage?

Third, the underground. I'm fed up with authors who find it necessary to drag in that good, old solution-solver. Have you any idea what an underground really is? I don't mean the bunch of protesters we've got with us now, but a real, hard, effective organisation, which presents a real threat to the government. They are rebels and as such would be crushed at no matter what cost by any form of government you can think of. But forget that. How the hell could a couple of relative aborigines teach them enough to enable them to rise and win a revolution just like that? What you are saying is that a couple of native Africans came paddling down the Hudson in a canoe and, before you can blink, have managed to teach our protesters their secrets and have overthrown the government. Possible? You tell me.'

'It could be done, darling.' The aging actress had been silent too long, 'you can't simply draw a line and say this can happen and this can't. I think Derek was perfectly right to write his play the way he did. And you forget the artistic connotations.'

'That,' said Rigby flatly, 'is a lot of crap and you know it. Artistic connotations my backside! I'm dealing with the logical development of stated premises. And I can prove it. Ralph! You tell them!'

'No,' said Ralph. 'Leave me out of this. It isn't my battle.'

'It's no battle,' insisted Rigby. 'Just tell them why his set-up couldn't be real.'

'You've already told them.' Ralph didn't want to get involved in a useless discussion. He caught Lavinia's eyes and shrugged. 'All right, then, have it your way.'

'You'll tell them?'

'Why not?' He looked at the staring faces. 'What John says is perfectly right. Every form of government, elite, aristocracy, power-group, call it what you like is basically interested in only one thing. That is the determination to stay in power. In order to do this they must disarm the populace. The reason is simple when you think about it. An armed population is a permanently rebellious one. The man who has the gun has the upper hand. In this day and age they've really succeeded.'

'Now wait a minute!' A man spoke up from the back of the crowd. 'What about the West? Two hundred years ago men went armed all the time.'

'The Wild West?' Rigby shrugged. 'The end of the nineteenth century, my friend, was the end of any pretence of democracy. Your pistol-toting cowboys lived at the end of an era. Europe was coming under the heel and we had to follow. Sure, men could buy and carry arms in the West — but how long did that state of affairs last? In England after the turn of the 20th Century a man couldn't buy or own a firearm without a police certificate and he needed another in order to buy ammunition. The act was extended to cover pneumatic weapons and in 1968 it included shotguns. Over here the Constitution guaranteed us certain rights — among them the right to bear arms — but that right has gone now, swallowed up by the Cavendish Enactment which grew from the English Offensive Weapons Act, which made it a crime to carry anything which could be used as a weapon. Guns, knives, clubs, umbrellas even. The deciding factor was how the police chose to take it. Now, if you walk down the street with a cane, you can be charged under the Enactment. So you see how stupid the premise of our young friend is? A totalitarian form of government with an armed populace simply couldn't exist. It wouldn't be permitted to exist. And the rest follows. Without arms how are you going to stage a rebellion? And, without a rebellion, the existing form of government will remain in power. Which, of course, is the whole point of the legislation.'

'Are you still talking about the play?' asked Ralph.

Rigby smiled. 'Of course. What else?'

'Nothing, it was just that — ' Ralph broke off as he felt the attention-signal from his wristwatch. 'Excuse me. I must make a call.'

It was the computer room at the 20th Precinct. The officer in charge smiled spitefully from the screen, relishing his small moment of revenge for past pressures. 'Sorry to bother you, Major, but we've had a murder report and the victim's on the files.' His face was replaced by a sheet of data. 'I thought you would like to be notified immediately. Inspector Frere is the local officer handling the routine investigation.'

'Thank you,' said Ralph noting the address. 'I'll leave right away.'

13

The city was all of spires, twisted minarets graceful as they reached towards the sky, bulbous onion-shapes decked with shimmering glitters, clean and slender towers lifting like hungry fingers gemmed and bright and glowing with colour. Pennants fluttered from the soaring pinnacles and a host of birds wheeled with flashing wings, dancing motes of music beating time to the celestial spheres.

On the plain below the city armies gathered, mailed and mounted men, faces blank behind shimmering steel, weapons lifted, plumes streaming, the sound of hooves and armour lifting in a muted chorus of destruction. Then shouts and screams and blood red and wetly glinting in the sun. Alone the victor strode into the city.

Servile men bowed low at his approach. Doors opened and women stared with bold, envious eyes. A chamber, red and black and filled with an amorphous monstrosity. A moist sucking and the scrape of scales. A sword, long and bright and sharply pointed. The thrust and wetness and the withdrawal to thrust again, and again, and again.

Scales vanished to be replace by soft and yielding flesh. The thrusting sword became himself.

Bored, he turned and the city vanished at a thought. Air whistled past his ears as he rose, soaring high so that the world shrank and became an insignificant ball. Floating in a sac of amniotic fluid he drifted through a universe of jewelled stars, arranging them into new and more pleasing configurations. His brain was a living coal, bursting with creative energy, entrancing concepts tumbling one over the other in a plethora of staggering thought. He was god and this was his universe to do with as he wished.

This was his heaven.

Stars flared to destruction as he flung one against another. Comets traced fiery trails and planets crisped to cinders in stellar furnaces. Galaxies wheeled to his mental command. All power and all destruction was his. All arrangement and all creation. There was nothing he could not do.

He was God.

For an infinity of time he floated and then, subtly, the universe changed. Somewhere something was beating with a monotonous rhythm. Something else sighed with a repetitive irritation. There was the sense of pressure and the fading and chaos ruled where before had been his supreme order. There was an impression of falling from tremendous heights and a smothering with mile upon mile of thick turgid slime.

Atwater groaned and slowly opened his eyes.

He stared at a ceiling covered with a mesh of lines so fine that they gave the impression of a spider's web. Light in tiny globules ran over and along the near-invisible strands vanishing when he tried to concentrate on any single gleam to reappear with tantalising vagueness when his attention wandered. The air itself seemed to be filled with drifting motes and wraiths of scratching unease. He closed his eyes and shuddered in vertigo, once again hearing the thudding beat of his heart, the sighing irritation of his breathing. Opening his lids he tasted dust and mucus in throat and mouth. His teeth were granite rocks roughened by endless time. A prickling fire lanced from a thousand tiny muscles and he had the sudden conviction that he was dead and bound in endless layers of linen bandage as if he were an Egyptian mummy stolen from some ancient tomb.

Dead but still able to feel pain and stiffness and a mounting, rebellious horror.

'No!'

The sound was that of tearing paper. Bandages cracked with puffs of dust, falling, vanishing as figments of his imagination as he lifted a hand to the agony of his throat. His lips were cracked and his tongue swollen, his windpipe a mass of sere and constricted tissue. He swallowed, painfully, abruptly aware of a raging thirst. Slowly he eased himself into an upright position.

He lay on a bed covered with imitation tiger-skin, the bed set on a floor of polished wood, the floor merging with walls decorated with silken paper in abstract designs. His own bed in his own room in his own apartment. Rising he staggered to where a door gave access to the bathroom and stooped over the washbasin. Water gushed from a faucet as he twisted the control and he plunged his face into the filling bowl. He drank, swallowing until his stomach was bloated and then, with reactive savagery, his body rejected the water in a gush of acrid vomit. He emptied the bowl and waited until it was clear before trying again, this time taking cautious sips and resisting the temptation to gulp. Raising his head he stared into the mirror and saw eyes lined with knighted circles, cheeks drawn, lips bloodless, the white bone prominent beneath his temple.

How long, he wondered. Two days? Five? Longer? How long could a man live without water? Atwater touched his stubbled cheeks conscious of hunger for the first time since he had been a boy. And that was as strange as his thirst.

Why should he feel either when he had eaten and drunk so well?

He drank again but something was wrong. The water didn't taste as it should and as he remembered. It had a flat, insipidity, a depressing lack of flavour, which did nothing for his taste buds and made drinking a chore.

Where were the sparkling dews of mountain streams? The exciting tang of sparkling rivers? The rich liquid that had laved the palate of a god?

Frowning, Atwater stripped off his robe and stepped into the shower. It's all right, he told himself. It's simply the reaction of a recent experience. There's nothing to worry about. Scented water lashed against his skin, a host of miniscule whips stinging the laggard blood to pulsing life. From the shower he stepped towards the air dryers and closed his eyes as the hot blasts dried his body with mechanical efficiency.

Where were the scented maidens with flower-petal hands? Softly smiling girls with silken hair and the warm velvet of yielding flesh, globular breasts tipped with spikes of coral and hips curved in an enticing sensuality? Fit handmaidens for the pleasure of a god.

The hot blast of air ceased and he looked into the full-length mirror as he turned from the machine. He paused at what he saw. A soft and paunchy body layered with fat instead of muscle, the genitals shrivelled and the skin like the wrinkled scab on sour milk. His jowls, accentuated by the stubble, hung like the dewlaps of a dog and his hair was a thin straggle plastered to his balding skull. Brown spots mottled the backs of his hands and the blue shadows of knotted veins writhed over his undeveloped calves.

Where was the strong and virile body he had known? Young and handsome with muscles of steel and skin like pliant leather? Tall and broad with a mane of hair rippling from forehead to shoulder. The body of a heroic god.

He shaved and dressed and combed his hair and, restless, strode into the lounge.

The contents of the cocktail cabinet did nothing to ease his disquiet, the alcohol and syrup and cunning blend of herb, failing to provide what the water lacked. Food was no better. The steak tasteless, the vegetable and sauces and side-dishes sent up from the restaurant below. He ate, it was fuel for his metabolism and a means to still the gnawing pain in his stomach, but like the water and wine it lacked the flavour he remembered.

Brooding he sat staring into a glass of brandy mixed with gin. Nectar and ambrosia, he thought. Once they have been tasted they can never be forgotten. And once a man has experienced what it means to be a god he can never forget the heady sense of euphoria such power can bring. Never forget and never be satisfied with anything less.

Swallowing the drink he looked at the ceiling. The web-like mash of lines had vanished, they had been a by-product of his post-drugged condition, but the intentional irregularities of the surface remained to catch little pockets of light and shadow, both an aid to concentration.

The way, he thought bleakly. The long, arduous, never-ending system of concentration and introspection during which a man was supposed to ponder on the mystery and meaning of the universe, sending his thoughts on a journey into inexplicable convolutions. And for what? So that he could begin to find the way to begin the endless journey towards the supreme state of bliss. The forever unattainable realm of Nirvana.

Impatiently he refilled his glass. What did they know about it those gurus who claimed to be infallible guides? If they could find the way as they claimed then why hadn't they taken it? Why remain among dirt and disease and aggressive contempt when they could step into a world of perpetual joy? And all the rest of them who preached of Heaven, why did they hang on to the very last fast if they believed in what they said? Would any man in his right mind stay in this stinking world if he had the means to escape?

The mixture was too warm and he went to get ice. The ice made it too weak so he added more spirit. And the drinks weren't doing as he'd hoped. Alcohol was a depressant and he was depressed enough and the more he drank the worse he felt. Irritable, he stared around the apartment. The colours were wrong, faded and dull when they should have been fresh and bright. The furnishing, the carpet, the paper on the walls, all looked tawdry and cheap. Even the sunlight coming through the windows looked dirty and stained.

God! What a lousy world in which to live!

He sat again, his mind toying with past glories as a man would remember a wonderful dream. And yet it had not been simply a dream, of that he was certain. Lovingly he recalled a stream of episodes, making comparisons, deriding those whom he had once envied.

The fighter in the stadiums — he too had seen steel and seen wounds gape and entrails gush and had felt the spurting warmth of released blood. And not once and not against a single opponent but many times against a host of foes. Lovers — he had wrung from them moans of satiated desire. Creation — he had built cities and fashioned worlds taking the universe apart like a child's toy and reassembling it into a pattern of his own devising.

He had done so much, perhaps too much, entranced with new world and his incredible powers. The next time he would be more restrained, taking time to savour things to the full and to wring from them the last scrap of enjoyment. It would take application and mental control but he had the trick of it now and wouldn't be so quickly overwhelmed with the sheer intoxication of being a God.

The next time, he thought. The next time.

Because there had to be a next time.

There had to be!

14

Against the row of decrepit shops the headquarters of the Society for the Preservation of Individual Liberties stood out like a painted thumb. It was all in blue and white with the letters SPIL traced in screaming red. The windows were painted and covered with signs reading KNOWLEDGE IS POWER! LEARN FOR LIBERTY! STUDY FOR SUCCESS! A small poster read PROCLAMATION! The large words followed by lines of text in 48pt type.

'We believe that the free and unrestricted disseminating of information is integral to the function of the democratic process and that any interference with the spread of knowledge is a betrayal of that process and the positive sign of the rule of dictatorship!'

Outside the shop a cluster of deadheads stood around, some leaning against the walls, others communing among themselves. Several wore a BEAT BIG BROTHER sash over their blue-denim coolie-like tunics and from across the street, it was impossible to tell the difference between male and female. As Ralph watched one of their number came from within the shop carrying a pile of leaflets and began distributing bundles of them around.

They were like ants, he thought, as they broke up and moved away. All dressed alike and with their hair exactly the same. A complete reversal from the time of his own youth when the young had tried desperately to achieve individuality by exotic raiment and, of course, had all ended by wearing a recognisable uniform. Now they had accepted the uniform and gloried in it. The sigma of the slave, the serf, the coolie. The young who had been exploited and pushed around by everyone from politicians to pushers. At least these kids had revolted finding their own life in their own way. Participation. A growing enclave within a community for which they held only contempt.

The shop held an open space flanked by a wide counter on which stood piles of leaflets. Behind the counter reared filing cabinets, mounds of papers and on desks computers and printing machines, the whole attended by a half-dozen deadhead workers. A girl, he could tell her sex by the timbre of her voice, spoke to him from behind the counter as he approached.

'Can I help you?'

'I want to see the man who runs this place.'

'I don't know what you mean.' Her eyes were wary, masked against intrusion. 'We all run it. The society is a commune.'

Ralph sighed and produced his identification. 'I'll put it another way. I want to see the man who took charge of the mail you have just had delivered.'

'Something wrong, Cherry?' A man, deeper voiced, older, came from the printing machine to stand at her side. He glowered at Ralph and at the badge he displayed. 'Police, uh? What's it this time? Rats in the walls? A new fire hazard? Too much noise? When are you guys going to leave us alone?'

'He wants to see Big Harry,' said the girl.

The man shrugged and jerked a thumb

towards a door in the rear. 'Then let him. Through there.

The door opened onto a room filled with the smell of damp and dust and paper. A wide desk was cluttered with proofs, layouts, artwork and finished products. More filing cabinets lined the walls and books lay everywhere. An old fashioned telephone, one without a screen, stood beside an electric stove bearing a percolator and a cot, unmade, rested against a wall. Ralph closed the door and looked at the man seated behind the desk.

He was a small man, wrinkled, his blue-denim hanging loosely on his emaciated frame. His hands and face were thin with prominent knuckles and bones. One eye hold a permanent squint and one ear held the earphone of a hearing aid. He was, Ralph guessed, at least sixty years of age.

'Are you Big Harry?'

The man smiled showing broken teeth. 'The work 'big' in this context means 'old'. But I wouldn't really say that I'm in charge. I'm just a stroller if you're particular about titles. I try to channel energy into productive lines and to eliminate waste.'

'And to spread information,' said Ralph dryly. 'I read your proclamation.'

'You disagree with it?'

'With the sentiments, no. With their execution, perhaps. It rather depends on what type of information you're spreading around. Some of it could fall into the wrong hands.'

'There speaks the Establishment,' said Harry smiling. 'And who determines which are the wrong hands? Whim, the Establishment, of course. Have you read the Alice books? If you have you'll know what I mean when I say that the Establishment always reminds me of Humpty Dumpty. You know — 'words mean what I want them to mean'. Could you, to satisfy my curiosity, define just what you mean by the 'wrong hands'?'

'Those who could use such information to break the law.'

'And who makes the law? Why the Establishment again. Well, well! Always we seem to return to the main point. The Establishment.' Big Harry gently shook his head. 'We aren't talking of God, you know. We are only talking about an institution of men who have taken it upon themselves to act as universal arbitrators of what we shall and shall not do. Why should their dictates be sacrosanct?'

'I didn't know they were,' said Ralph. He looked around and saw a chair loaded with books. Removing them he sat down.

'Laws are made to protect the common weal but there is nothing sacred about them. They can be changed, and those against gambling and lotteries and prostitution, together with private knife-fights and other spectacles. All are legal now on the basis that they are consentient acts between adults in private. But the Establishment never yields one iota of its power. As it apparently eases in one direction it clamps down in another with a host of new legislation. But, as a policeman, you must know that. Coffee?'

Ralph blinked at the abrupt change of subject. 'No thank you.'

'It's quite good,' said Big Harry rising to help himself. He moved awkwardly because of a stiffened knee. 'We have friends in Brazil who keep us supplied.'

'I imagine you have friends everywhere,' said Ralph. 'Chemists, for example?'

'Possible.'

'I'm thinking of one in particular. A man named Olsen. Jorge Olsen. He wrote to you.'

Big Harry smiled. 'He did?'

'You've got the letter on your desk from him. I want to see any others he might have sent.'

'My dear friend, help yourself.' Big Harry waved his mug of coffee at the filing cabinets. 'Go through everything with a fine comb. You've done it before, often, but I'll tell you now that you won't find anything because there isn't anything to find. We don't keep names and addresses and lists of members. If people want to help the society they send what they can, paper, machinery, money for food and rent and things like that. Labour and operating costs as regards distribution are free. We don't use real names because they are labels of the Establishment, instead we call ourselves anything we choose. But you know all this. Your police agents have infiltrated us as they have every other group regarded by the Establishment as being undesirable to their policy.'

Ralph didn't comment on the obvious truth of the statement. Instead he said, 'And this information you disseminate? How is it received?'

'People send us things, anonymously, of course, items which they consider to be of interest and which, peculiarly, are not available in the public libraries. Things like this.' He gestured toward the litter on the desk. 'Help yourself.'

Ralph picked up a leaflet.

WARNING!

The manufacture of explosives is illegal and dangerous. Do NOT grind any compound containing sugar and sodium chlorate — an ingredient of many weed-killers — as friction and or concussion with . . .

He put it down and picked up another. This one carried a detailed sketch of a human throat with marked pressure point. It read:

BEWARE!

The carotid arteries are situated in the neck as illustrated and carry blood directly to the brain. Pressure on these arteries can cause rapid unconsciousness and, if the pressure is continued, death. A defence against such an attack is the wearing of a high collar or some stiff material.

'Nice,' said Ralph, putting it down. 'You are telling people how to make bombs and to use Karate.' He picked up another of the leaflets. It contained a list of domestic chemicals that could be used to make a delayed action incendiary device. Yet another listed proscribed drugs and their vegetable origins — and a warning against home extraction of the active ingredients and, of course, telling how it should not be done. Others contained details on how to make a radio-jamming device, eye-irritating smoke, fulminates, abrasive fluids, guncotton, gunpowder, cordite, how to by-pass electric and gas meters, to cheat the pay-phones and to get the best from welfare. All accompanied in big letters by warnings that to do any of these things was strictly against the law.

All of them, on the reverse sides, contained information on shopping bargains, mostly a list of domestic drugs with both their trade and generic names and the savings to be made by purchasing the latter.

'The drug houses must love you,' said Ralph dryly as he studied the details. 'Is this the hook to catch the housewife?'

'They appreciate the information. And it isn't against the law to tell someone how to save money. Nor how to defend themselves.'

'Karate is a proscribed sport.'

'True, but there are karate clubs as there are gun clubs even if every weapon has to be registered and they have to account for every round fired. None of that information is illegal and you note, we give full warning as to the legality of what we describe.'

'A cover,' said Ralph. 'And you know it. What you are really doing is to teach people how to make things that can be used to hurt and injure. Bombs, explosives, incendiary devices, all the rest of it.'

'Information you will not find in any library,' said Big Harry quietly. 'I said it was peculiar that it couldn't be found but, of course, it isn't that at all. The lack of such information is due to deliberate censorship. I've seen it happen during my lifetime. When I was young any kid could get a book on how to make fireworks. Now such books are only available to those authorised to use professional libraries. Then came the internet, and for nearly fifty years there was total freedom — anything and everything could be put out on websites that anyone with a p.c. could view. They can't now. No one can. All internet providers are state controlled and the present system used enables the Cyber Police to track and, if they don't like it, to block what everyone views or transmits. The Establishment justified their action on the grounds that they were able to stop the activities of paedophiles — '

'And you regard that as a bad thing?'

'Of itself, no, but it was only a cloak for their *real* agenda, which was to control and suppress personal freedom. I regard all censorship as bad. I regard the deliberate repressing of information as a direct attack on the liberty of the individual. And it doesn't stop with not letting people know how to make things which could possibly be used to escalate riots and lead to rebellion. It is refusing to tell them of their rights under the law such as they are. A calculated policy of intimidation by ignorance. A cop walks in here and throws his weight around. I do not know, because I am not allowed to know, just what right he has to demand what he does? Should he have a search warrant? Am I allowed to call a lawyer? Need I when he says no simply because he wears a uniform and a badge? Just what are the police supposed to be, anyway?'

'A force to implement the law,' said Ralph quietly. 'A body of men to detect crime and to apprehend the criminals. To prevent crime if they can and to guard the public always.'

'Servants, then?'

'Yes.'

'With a set of rules they are supposed to follow?'

'Yes, the police are not above the law.'

'And how am I to know if they are following their own rules if I'm not allowed to know what they are?' Big Harry shook his head. 'You're talking of an ideal not things as they are. The police don't consider themselves as the servants of the public but as their masters. They've got the uniform, the badge, the club and gun. Knights among the peasants. Not for you, perhaps, you've got money and influence and the right kind of social background. And that's not counting your job. But for us? People who haven't any of these things?'

Big Harry leaned across the desk, his thin face intent. 'Listen. A cop could walk in here and shoot me dead. All he has to do is to put a gun or knife in my desk and say he thought I was going for it. Not even that. He could take me and smash in my skull and then say I was resisting arrest. And he would be believed or at least, permitted to get away with it. Who is going to argue? Where are the witnesses? What cop is going to accuse one of his own? Protect the public? My friend, you would make me laugh if the whole thing wasn't so damned tragic.' He saw Ralph's expression.

'You don't believe me? You think I'm exaggerating? Then answer me this. How many murdered are avenged? How many people robbed and beaten ever get their money back or see their attackers brought to court? How many crimes of violence are there every single day?'

'Too many,' admitted Ralph. 'But the police are doing what they can. There simply aren't enough of them to do it all. Crowd control, riot control, traffic and queue control — '

'Control,' interrupted the man behind the desk. 'That's the operative word. The police now are used as an instrument to control the public. Troops would be a little too raw and destroy the phoney image of democracy cultivated by the Establishment. Democracy! That's another laugh. A man gets the chance to vote once every now and again and they call it democracy! When did we ever have a referendum to discover what we, the majority, really want? I'll tell you, never. And we never will. All we get the chance to do is vote which of a handful of parties will take power and they're so much the same that's no damn choice at all. And when we try to protest about it what happens? You've said it. Control Gas and guns and water cannon. Arrest on suspicion and detention without trial. I know. I've been through it. A kneecap smashed and an elbow broken. A club in the groin and another which smashed an ear. But we learn, my friend. We learn. Now you can come in here whenever you like and look at anything you want. No secret lists of sympathisers. No names. No resistance. We get harassed, of course, when your precious police come in but we can live with it. We have to. We've got no choice.'

'That isn't quite true,' said Ralph. 'You've always got a choice.'

'Get out?' Big Harry nodded, sombre as he looked at his hands. 'I've thought about it,' he admitted. 'Often. One eye's gone and I like to read and watch sunsets and, even at my age, look at a pretty girl. Another tangle with the police and I could end up blinded for life. But you just can't give in. If you've got any spunk at all you've got to keep fighting. This society is mad and sick and wrong to hell. The young can see it but we can't leave it all to them. We've got to help if we can in any way we're able! But, Christ, man! Don't you think that at my age I want to rest?'

He wouldn't, of course. He couldn't. Not until he was dead. Natural-born revolutionaries are like that.

15

'Nice, huh?' Bastedo was a brightly-dressed monkey crouched in the dim alcove of the night club. He looked towards the singer as she sat at her piano his lips moist with secret thoughts. 'Look at that figure. Man, did you ever see such development? Plenty of handling went into shaping those curves, I'll bet. That's what you call a real, man-sized woman.'

Kelman toyed with his drink. He was beginning to regret that he had kept the rendezvous at Mother Hastings's place but after the girl had run off with his money he'd had little choice. He could have gone into business, he supposed, but caution had warned him against it. Instead he had accepted Bastedo's charity and now was beginning to pay for it. But not for much longer, he decided. Tonight they would get down to business or he would pull out.

'Listen,' he said. 'We've got to — ' He

broke off as the singer commenced another song, sitting as the warm liquid of her voice lapped around him, the piano a barely necessary accompaniment to the sheer beauty of her vocal magic. Like all her songs it held a poignancy that hurt all the more because only faintly understood. As applause rose in a crashing thunder he looked at his companion. 'Give me a bill. A big one.'

Bastedo blinked. 'Say! Are you going to — '

'The money!'

She turned her face towards him as he thrust through the crowd around the piano, joining those who were expressing their appreciation of her art by stuffing bills between her capacious breasts.

'You, man! What are you doing?'

'Showing my pleasure.'

'With money?'

He felt the silence around him, the sudden watchfulness of her friends. 'Yes.'

'Come closer,' she ordered, and her hands, delicate petals tipped with rose, lifted to touch his face. 'You're different,' she crooned. 'I can smell it. You're a bird that's been cooped up too long. Now you're free and itching to fly. Fly straight, man. Fly straight.'

Tension relaxed as he looked into her face. The old injuries were there, the white scars on the ebon skin, the shielding lenses, bearing her wounds like a tattered flag of an ancient war. But, even with them, she was beautiful.

'Take back your money, man,' she said. 'I've got money. I eat and sleep and take a drink at times. I've got friends — can you say as much? But what I need I haven't got. That's heaven, man. Heaven. You want to please me you bring me heaven.' Her voice rose, high, demanding. 'You all hear that? You want to please me then you bring me heaven.'

'Sure, Linda!' called a man. 'Coming right up on a plate!'

'Give us Stormy Weather, Linda!'

'Make it Yesterday's Lover!'

'How about Eyes of Peeling, Touch of Sight?'

'Yea, Linda! How about that?'

Kelman returned to his table as she struck up the requested number. Bastedo looked cynically over the edge of his glass.

'Feel better now, boy scout?'

Kelman grunted, not wanting to talk about it, wondering a little at his action. It had just seemed the right thing to do. He threw down the returned bill. 'Here's your money.'

'Keep it.'

'You may as well take it. She didn't need it.'

'So she flung it right back in your face.' Bastedo shrugged. 'Well, you heard what she said. You know what she wants. Get it and you'll be number one on her social register.'

Kelman frowned. 'Get what?'

'You don't know? God, but you're dumb. It's a name for the stuff, man. The real stuff. That's what she was asking for. Heaven.'

'I've been three years in a coop,' said Kelman tightly. 'You know what it's like in Dexter. If this stuff is new I wouldn't know about it. Maybe you'd better explain.'

Bastedo finished his drink. 'Sure. But not here. Let's go somewhere private.'

They talked in a subway, huddled at one end of a car, their voices almost drowned in the rattle of wheels, the pneumatic hiss of doors. The small man was Eve offering temptation and, like Adam, Kelman fell.

'All right,' he said finally. 'Count me in.'

'You're willing to go all the way?' Bastedo was insistent. 'Kill if you have to?'

Kelman looked down at his hands, thinking of Dexter, the girl who had left him, the life he faced without money.

'Yes,' he said flatly. 'What have I got to loose?'

They changed cars and left the subway walking down streets thick with the dusk of approaching night. A door gave onto stairs, the stairs to a room. Silhouetted against a window the girl was all shadow and vagueness, dark hair over a too-pale face, the skin of throat and breasts a soiled whiteness against the edges of an open robe. She turned as they entered, smoke pluming from a dangling cigarette.

'Sam?'

'That's right,' said Bastedo. 'And this is

Jack. We shared bed and board together.'
He approached the window.

'Is anything cooking?'

'Not that I noticed.' The girl's voice
was flat, harsh with a grating inflexion.
'What's so special about the store, Sam?
Why pay me to watch it? Have you got a
sudden yen for candy?'

Questions, thought Bastedo, savagely.
Always questions. These goddam whores
had too much curiosity. Quickly he said.
'Better than that, Wanda. The old guy's
dead, right? The police have lost interest.
What do they care about one more
murder? So what's wrong with us moving
in and taking over?'

She thought about it for a moment
then shrugged. 'I guess it's one way to get
a roof. You move in and everyone's going
to think that you did it legal. Unless the
old man has heirs who is going to ask
questions?' She held out her hand. It
was slim with the nails sharpened and
pointed to the semblance of claws. Vicious
weapons in case of need. 'You promised
me a hundred for keeping watch,' she
said. 'Give.'

Bastedo passed over the money, watched as she tucked it into the top of her stocking with a flash of thigh. 'You're certain there's no one still hanging around?'

'I've been watching since you told me,' she said. 'There's no one in there. Give it a while longer and the kids will move in and strip the place. If they don't the squatter will.' She looked at Kelman. 'You look a little restless, honey. Maybe I could do something about that.'

'Forget it,' said Bastedo. 'We haven't the time. Let's get on with the job.'

The door of the store was locked, the latch breaking as Kelman applied his weight. From somewhere in the dark interior a bell jangled. Kelman froze.

'It's all right,' said Bastedo. 'It's rigged to the door so as to signal when anyone opens it. Olsen spent most of his time in the rear.' He stepped inside the store and closed the door behind Kelman. 'Find something to jam it solid. We don't want to be interrupted.'

In the living room, the lights on, the door shielding their glow from the outside, he looked at the expensive furniture and frowned.

The frown deepened as they entered the bedroom and he found the concealed projector.

'Something wrong?' Kelman turned from watching a nubile young girl fighting a losing battle for her maidenhead with a burglar who had surprised her in the bath.

'This!' Bastedo slammed his hand against the control and the couple, locked in a frozen embrace, vanished from the wall. 'Six months ago Olsen didn't have a thing. A crummy ex-con scraping a living and broke all the time. But he was a chemist and a good one and I talked him into taking a chance. I staked him with almost everything I had. He was to make the stuff and I'd handle the distribution. Then I got picked up on that lousy offensive weapons charge and got sent to Dexter. When I came out everything seemed fine but I wanted a little help. Your muscle in case I ran into something I couldn't handle. Then what? Olsen gets himself shot. I was lucky that I didn't run into the police. I found Wanda and hired her to keep an eye on things.'

'So?'

'I figured that he'd gone into production and that the stuff would be hidden away. Now I'm not so sure. He's been spending and doing it heavy. He must have known that I'd been picked up and probably decided to enjoy himself. That or he got scared.'

'You can't be sure of that,' protested Kelman. He sat on the edge of the bed, thinking, fighting his disappointment. Bastedo had made it all sound so easy but he should have known better. No fortune ever came easy. Always it had to be worked for. 'He had money,' he said. 'The stuff he brought proves that. Maybe he did get into production and try it on his own. Or maybe he found another backer. The shooting could have been anything. Some kid wanting to rob the till and getting scared, perhaps..'

'It's possible,' said Bastedo. 'And it's what I figure must have happened. But all this stuff makes a difference. He could have bumped up against some of the big operators and they didn't like the competition.'

'Six months isn't long.' Kelman was grimly following his own train of thought. 'It would take time for him to set up production. And if he had run up against the big boys they wouldn't have killed him. He was a good investment and they would have taken him over. How did he sound when you approached him?'

'Riding high,' admitted Bastedo. 'Full of beans.'

'Then he wasn't afraid of you. That means he must have had something to show.'

'That's right!' Bastedo's optimism had returned. He slammed his hand on the headboard of the bed and said, 'The police came while he was still warm. I've had the place watched all the time and no one has touched it since they left. To them it was a routine stick-up murder and they wouldn't have looked beyond their noses. The stuff must still be here. All we have to do is find it. Just as I said.'

Kelman nodded, watching the wall, the triggered projectors painting the smooth expanse with colour and frenetic activity.

16

At times Ralph thought of the place as a cathedral, a regulated expanse of shining efficiency filled with dedicated servitors of the surrogate brains housed in their sterile shrines. The new priests of the new God of unlimited memory and infallible response. Even the aura of sanctity was there as if the stored details of numerous lives had somehow acquired a separate tangibility. Libraries, he remembered, had once given him the same impression. A feeling of primitive awe in the face of so much accumulated knowledge.

'Major Mancini?' The girl was young and smiling yet appearing oddly detached in the white isolation of her uniform.

'I'm sorry that you've been kept waiting, sir, but Major Thorne is ready to see you now.'

'Good.' Ralph climbed stiffly from his chair.

'You look tired, sir. Could I get you anything? Coffee? Tea?'

'No thank you.' He returned her smile. 'Just lead me to the Major.'

Thorne was the man in charge of the 20th Precinct computer room, the High Priest of the Machine. He gestured Ralph to a chair as he entered the office and pursed his lips as he studied a sheaf of papers he picked up from his desk.

'I must tell you, Major,' he said acidly, 'that this personal interview seems to me to be entirely unnecessary. The results of the investigation you requested could have easily been dispatched direct to your own office. I tell you, frankly, I resent this disruption of normal procedure.'

Ralph remembered to be diplomatic. 'Look,' he said, 'Let's not fight like two cocks on a dunghill. We've both had a long day but I'm trying to stop something before it can get really started. Also,' he added, 'I wanted your specialised knowledge on certain matters. To have passed e-mails backwards and forwards would waste the time of us both.' He leaned forward to look at the papers. 'Is that the report on the paper we found in Olsen's store?'

'It is.' Thorne, a little mollified by Ralph's appreciation of the importance of his labours, passed it over. 'As you see the Formula is undoubtedly that for the manufacture of MDM. However it was not written by Olsen. No other paper of this type was found in the store and the configurations of the writing are definitely not his. The inference is that he received it from some outside source. The envelope was addressed by him, we have specimens of his handwriting for purpose of comparison, of course, but not the formula.'

Ralph frowned. 'It was not a copy, of course?'

'No.' Thorne riffled more papers. 'The samples you sent from the SPIL offices have all tested negative. No writing is similar to that on the formula. Not,' he pointed out, 'that it would have helped if they had. All were anonymous.'

'It's the way they work,' said Ralph mildly. He remembered the envelopes he had opened. They had contained nothing but donations or items of information. In no case had there been an address or a signature of meaning. 'They don't keep files or records. They take in what is sent and check it against information they already have. If it's duplicated they just throw it away. If not they take down the details and burn the original. The rest is a matter of publication and distributing.'

'Incredible!' Thorne's neat mind was shocked at the concept of such disorder. 'How can any organisation operate without records?'

'They can and they do,' said Ralph. 'It's the new system. If anyone wants to join in they simply do that. If they want to drop out they can. I had it all explained to me. When you think about it it's really quite efficient. From their point of view, naturally.'

Better than the cell systems of the old revolutionaries, he thought as Thorne riffled his papers. Now, if the police took in a deadhead for questioning, he would tell all he know and it wouldn't matter because there was nothing he could really tell. Some ideals that were common knowledge anyway. No apparent leaders. No inflicted discipline. Could any revolution ever hope to succeed on such a basis?

He remembered Rigby's conception of an underground but the critic has been thinking in terms of the past. The new rebellion had no recognisable form and, logically, it couldn't have if it hoped to succeed. Established forms of government were too well aware of the traditional forms of resistance and knew exactly how to deal with them. Instead the new underground had a formless, amorphous quality, a dozen different groups interlinked and overlapping but each a separate entity and all working towards the same, simple end. Not to achieve personal power but simply to corrode the existing order by ceaseless antagonism. BEAT BIG BROTHER! Beat the Establishment by refusing to automatically obey each and every command. Refuse to toe the line because you were told to do it. Ignore the welter of official forms demanding personal details. Question every order and insist on every right. Use the existing framework as a weapon against itself as the old strikers used to do when they 'worked to rule'. Refuse, always, to cooperate.

Cultivate a cynicism, an indifference and a deliberate return to a more primitive form of life.

Weapons against which a society that depended on endless sales and deliberately contrived envy would be economically helpless.

'Major?'

Ralph blinked, conscious that he had been mentally drifting and had almost fallen asleep. 'I'm sorry. You were saying?'

'The formula does not match the handwriting of anyone working at the MDM manufacturing plant. If it originated there it has been copied by an unknown hand.'

'How about the handwriting of those isolated on the initial run-through?'

'Negative. There hasn't been time to run a thorough check but what results we have obtained are inconclusive.' Thorne cleared his throat. 'I'm sorry, Major. I'm afraid that we have gone as far as we can on the basis of the data supplied. Would you care for my comments?'

'Please.'

'There are too many intangibles. The information could have been obtained from a number of professional publications and it is impossible to check all available sources. Agreed that those who would have had access to such publications are limited yet their numbers are still vast.'

'It doesn't follow,' said Ralph mildly. 'We are concerned with someone who, for reasons of their own, wanted to disseminate the means of manufacturing MDM. Chemists with a record of dissatisfaction with the present government, perhaps. Liberals with pronounced views of the gratifying legislation appertaining to drug-control and censorship. That could narrow the field.'

'But not enough, I'm afraid. And, if as I suspect the formula has been copied, what possible proof could we have?'

It was a dead end but Ralph wasn't too disappointed. To have hoped for an easy solution would have been to have asked for a miracle and he was policeman enough to have learned the necessity of patience. It was a thing that had had to be done, and elimination of probabilities if nothing else, a part of the endless attention to detail which was a part of the job.

He sat back, thoughtful, giving his trained instincts free rein. This was where the human element beat the massed computers. They could only work from the basis of known data, extrapolation from ascertained fact, but intuition worked on a different level.

'I'd like you to run a work-association check on those leaflets I sent you from SPIL,' he said to Thorne. 'A comparison-test as to phraseology and punctuation. I'll let you have the names of those whom I want checked out. It's possible there is a relationship there which could be of use.'

Thorne raised his eyebrows. 'It will take time, Major. Our schedule is pretty tight as it is.'

'I realise that. I will keep the list short and I'm not going to breath down your neck.' Ralph smiled, striving to gain the other's willing cooperation. 'It's a thin hope but it may give me a lead and, frankly, I need all the help I can get. The way I see it is this. As you pointed out it will be impossible to check all those who have had access to the relevant information. We have to track back-wards from Olsen and SPIL.'

Thorne frowned. 'But why SPIL? I realise the envelope was addressed to them but you didn't find a copy of the formula in their files, did you?'

'No, and I doubt if they have received one yet. It could have gone to any of their other offices in the large cities but I doubt it. I'm having them checked just in case but I'll be surprised if we find it.'

'Your reasons?'

'The formula is an intricate one. I think that Olsen was given the job of checking it out and, if possible, to simplify it. When he'd done as he was to have posted it to SPIL. He was killed before he could do it.'

'Or he may not have intended to do it at all,' said Thorne musingly. He shook his head. 'What kind of a man would deliberately spread information of such a nature? He must be insane.'

'The dedicated often are,' said Ralph dryly. 'From our viewpoint, of course, not theirs.'

'I suppose he deludes himself that he is aiding the cause of freedom,' said Thorne disgustedly. Freedom! You might as well give a chick acid and guns to play with. The public has to be protected against such men. Such information is dangerous!'

'All knowledge is potentially dangerous,' said Ralph quietly. 'That of how to make fire, for example. And yet without such knowledge how would we hope to progress?'

'There is a difference — information of scientific discovery which is, and should be, retained for scientific personnel only, and that which is released for public consumption.' Thorne was sharp, a scientist defending his privileged position as one of the elite. 'It takes skill and training in order to evaluate such information and to use it in constructive ways. It must not be allowed to fall into irresponsible hands. In any case the information as to MDM is classified. Surely they know that if they disseminate it they will be breaking the law?'

'Perhaps, but I don't think that will stop them,' said Ralph. 'In any case, to be fair, how are they to know that it is classified unless we tell them? To an ordinary man one chemical formula looks much like another.'

'Ignorance is no excuse. And how can we tell them? If we do that they will know exactly what it is we are trying to keep secret.'

'That's right,' said Ralph dryly. 'It's a question of the chicken and the egg. They mustn't use it because it will break the law if they do. But, equally so, they mustn't be allowed to know what it is they mustn't use because then they'll have information we don't want them to have. Sometimes it seems as if we can't win.'

But that wasn't true, he thought as he left the office and headed towards the elevator. The police, the Establishment, would always win because they had the power of law and the law was what they chose to make it. A stick with which to beat down any opposition. Retroactive legislation, if nothing else, could always do the job. A man then could be charged with having performed a criminal act when, at the time he had done it, had been legal.

The public didn't stand a chance.

17

Down in the foyer Ralph felt a touch on his arm and turned to see Hilda Hickstead at his side. The attorney looked tired, dark circles beneath her eyes, the pallor of her face ghastly beneath the carefully applied cosmetics.

'Hello, Major Mancini,' she said. 'Still on duty?'

'Ralph,' he corrected. 'I'm just going off. And you?'

'The same.' She fell silent and he wondered why she had approached him and then, in an obvious effort to make conversation, she said, 'You look tired. Has it been a hard day?'

'I've been on the go since yesterday morning but you get used to long hours in my job. And what about yourself? You look all in.'

'I'm the only one on call now,' she said. 'And they keep ringing.'

Ralph shrugged. 'Then let them ring.

You're not their servant.'

'I'm what they pay for,' she said with mild reproof. 'Legal help when they need it. It's just that there are so many of them and they will keep getting arrested.'

'If they're in jail they can wait,' he said curtly. 'A few hours in a cell won't hurt them. And, anyway, what can you do? You're letting them lean on you too hard. You'll have to grow a thick skin and a callous disposition or you'll go under.'

'No.' She took a deep breath. 'It's just that I'm tired. Things will look different in the morning.'

'Perhaps,' he said dryly. 'They usually do.' He looked at her, noting the neat helmet of her dark hair, the slender line of her throat. Her breasts were hidden by the severe lines of her suit but nothing could disguise the feminine lines of her hips and thighs. He said, 'Is Captain Markham giving all the help you need?'

'Yes, thank you.'

He doubted it. The captain was one of the old school, short on both imagination and patience. He would do his job but would refuse to extend himself more than he had to. In his eyes Hilda, because she represented those arrested, would be one of the 'enemy'. A troublemaker who insisted on rocking the boat. Almost he decided to have a word with the captain then thought better of it. It didn't pay to interfere and it was none of his business.

But why had she approached him in the first place? She's lonely, he thought, with sudden insight. Fresh to the job and a little overwhelmed by the sheer magnitude of it all. She had reached out, instinctively, to a known face and was now probably regretting it.

He said, 'Has it ever occurred to you that most of your clients are phonies? That the cards they carry aren't genuine?'

'Forgeries, you mean?'

'Yes. It doesn't take much to copy a Defence card. Any of a hundred underground printers could do it. Have you any means of checking?'

'We have. But with the staff position what is is — '

'You don't,' he ended for her. 'You take these applicants at face value. No wonder they hold us all in such contempt.' He smiled at her outraged expression. 'Now before you get on your high horse and tell me how noble these deadheads are just remember that I've been on the job a lot longer than you have and so can fairly claim to know them a little better than you do. Of course they use forged cards if they can get them. Why not? They don't consider they owe you anything and they have no intention of paying for something they can get for free or for less than face value. I could get you a hundred of your cards at a dollar each. That's four hundred dollars you'd lose right away. No wonder Defence can't afford a decent staff as well.' He broke off.

'Or an experienced attorney,' he said. 'Someone who knows all the ropes. Like Max. He had a gutful before he decided to quit.' He took her arm. 'Anyway, let's not talk about it standing here. Where do you live?'

'The Montage Apartments.'

'Snap,' he said. 'So do I. Let's share a cab.'

Cushioned in the dark interior her face was a pale blur illuminated with coloured flashes of passing light. The driver, assuming they were lovers, kept silent for which both were grateful. After a while she said, 'Ralph, why do they do it?'

'The deadheads?'

'All of them. Why do they take drugs?'

'Why does a man hit the bottle? For escape. They don't like the world as it is or they can't face it and so they duck out from under. Do you drink?'

She smiled. 'I've been known to get high on special occasions.'

'Then you know how it is. After a few drinks you begin to unwind a little, to relax. Things don't seem to be quite the same. The edge isn't so sharp. Worries aren't as overpowering as they were and you get a 'what-the-hell' attitude towards life.'

'Until the glow dissipates,' she reminded. 'Until the time of the hangover.'

'Sure, and then you take a few more drinks to recapture the sense of well-being. That's what makes a dipsomaniac. They can't bear to face reality and so keep drinking in order to escape from it. They do it to excess, true, but it could happen to any of us. We are all potential dipsomaniacs. We can never be sure that the bottle won't get us in the end.'

'You're being pessimistic,' she said. 'And exaggerating. One drink and then destruction.'

'It happens,' he said shortly. 'Too damned often. The bottle is always there, always tempting, always offering a release from tension and a way out. Chronic drunkenness is one of our biggest social problems.'

'Together with under housing, over-population and lack of education,' she admitted. 'I know that. But surely it isn't the same as drug addiction?'

He sighed. 'Unfortunately it is, Hilda. The addicts take dope for exactly the same reason a dipsomaniac takes alcohol. In order to escape a world they do not like and can't even begin to alter. And, like a dipsomaniac, when they come out of their glow and hit the hangover they have to take more. And more. And more. You can't cure them because you can't alter the situation that made them turn to drugs in the first place. They find the world bearable only while they can alter their viewpoint of it. They change the world within their heads because they can't change it outside. Simple.'

'And cowardly.'

'No,' he said thoughtfully, 'I don't think you can honestly say that. It isn't really cowardice to run from what you don't like. A lack of adjustment, perhaps, but what real virtue is there in suffering? If there was we would still refuse to use anaesthetics in surgery. If there is virtue in pain then all of us would seek it. You know what they call that?'

'Masochism.' Her eyes gleamed red as the cab halted at a stop sign, the ruby light reflecting from her pupils. 'You're a strange man, Ralph. I could almost believe that you sympathise with those I represent.'

'Don't.' The cab moved forward and turned a corner, the movement throwing him towards her so that he had to extend his hand to prevent a collision. Beneath his palm he felt the warmth and softness of her yielding thigh. 'I can understand why they do it but that doesn't mean I agree with what they do. And it's my job to stop it regardless of how I might feel. They are breaking the law and that's all there is to it.'

He swayed again as the cab made another turn then braked before the block of apartments. Ralph climbed out and helped the woman, catching a glimpse of her long, curved legs, the thick roundness of her thighs as they joined the smooth enticement of her hips. Paying the cabbie he led the way into the apartment.

'Which floor are you?'

'The eighth,' she said. 'And you?'

'Right up high. The thirty-second.'

'Close to the stars.' She smiled and held out her hand. 'It was nice meeting you. One day I'll ask you to join me in a special occasion so that we can tempt the demon alcohol together. In the meantime thank you for bringing me home.'

It was neatly done, he thought as she walked towards the elevator. A clean, quick break that left an opening for the future if he wished to take advantage of it. Or perhaps he was mistaken and the whole thing had been a matter of a casual meeting and nothing more. Idly he wondered what awaited her upstairs. A Man of the Month, perhaps? A temporary husband to take off her shoes and to massage her feet and to bring her a reviving drink. Someone who kept house and who would reach out and touch her hair and implement her need to be assured of her own, individual value to the world.

Probably not, he thought, riding up in the cage of his own elevator. She would be going home to books and files and sheaves of paper. To sigh and struggle with the problems of others, sublimating her own needs in a mountain of work. And yet she was a woman and an attractive one. It was gratifying to think that she had found him pleasant company.

He heard music as he opened the door of his apartment, loud, brassy, spilling with harsh discordance a modern work by a modern composer, lacking all the subtle grace of the old masters.

'Ralph?'

'That's right.'

'I'll be with you in a second, darling!'

The voice was strange as the woman was strange. She came running towards him from the kitchen, a wealth of blonde hair, luminous blue eyes, breasts which bounded like grapefruit beneath the soft texture of a robe. She reached him and closed her arms around his neck. Her lips were soft and full and demanding. Her body full of heat.

'Ralph, darling, you're so wonderfully handsome,' she said. 'Lavinia told me you were but I thought she must be exaggerating. Now I see that she wasn't.' She stepped back, smiling. 'I'm Sophia. I'm sure that we're going to be very happy.'

'Lavinia?'

'She's gone, silly! Did you forget the date? I'm sure that you wouldn't want us both around.' Her tone was warm, intimate. 'Now you sit down while I get you a drink.'

It was his usual, of course, it would be. He sat nursing it, adjusting to the new situation, angry at himself for having been taken unawares. At first when he'd signed on with the agency he'd looked forward each month to the new arrivals, eager to learn what new surprises were in store. Then he had become blasé and later he had grown resentful of change. And Lavinia?

He hadn't even wished her farewell.

He finished his drink and Sophia was at his side.

'Hungry, darling? I've a nice casserole in the oven. I wasn't sure what time you'd be home so I had to get something that would stay hot without spoiling.'

'Thank you, dear,' he said. 'But I'm not hungry.'

'Another drink then?'

'Please.'

She crossed to the makings and returned with two glasses, sitting at his side, eyes bright as she sipped at her drink. Remembering she rose and switched off the radio. The enchanting strains of Stravinsky drifted from the stereo, and soothed him with familiar sound.

'You look tired, darling,' she murmured returning to the couch and snuggling close at his side. 'Had a hard day?'

He nodded, still thinking of Lavinia and the domestic events of the day. She would have waited for her successor in order to give her a quick briefing on the layout of the apartment and his personal habits. She might even have discussed his sexual peculiarities, his dislike of spoken obscenities, intimate details which a wife should know. Then she would have gone — to where? A new man, a new home, a fresh experience. Was she, at this very moment, stooping over a stranger, treating him like a husband and offering a drink and consolation?

Irritably he shook his head, conscious of Sophia's eyes and knowing that he was being unfair. As she was his new bride so he was her new husband. This was their honeymoon and ghosts had no place in their nuptial bed.

18

In the city a thing was screaming.

It shrieked with the blind incoherence of an animal so badly hurt that nothing mattered but to make sound, noise, cries which echoed through the canyons and gullies of the artificial jungle. A formless, pleading call for help and understanding which bounced from towers and cliffs of serried windows, the blank faces of uncaring concrete.

Ralph woke, sweating, conscious of the phone ringing at the side of the bed. He ignored it, waiting for the hammering of his heart to ease, nerves crawling with the aftermath of nightmare. Beside him Sophia moved, restless, her naked arms enfolding his nudity. The heat from her body was a sensual flame.

'Darling,' she murmured sleepily. 'I love you, darling. I love you.'

Momentarily he yielded to the embrace, finding comfort in the softness of her woman's flesh.

The phone kept ringing.

'Darling!' she turned, blonde hair damp against her face, eyes sleepy as she fought the external world of ceaseless interruptions. 'Turn it off, darling.'

Reluctantly he pulled away, rising to reach the instrument, blinking in the sudden light from the screen. A UNLEA operator looked at him, an unconscious voyeur, the focus of the scanners not reaching to the other side of the bed.

'Major Mancini?'

'Speaking.'

'A report from the lab, Major. You asked to be notified immediately the neurological study of Olsen's brain has been completed.'

'That's right,' admitted Ralph. 'So I did.'

'Your orders, Major?'

'Arrange for a showing in thirty minutes. You'd better contact Inspector Frere and ask him to be present. Ask, not order, be polite.'

'As you say, Major. Anything else?'

'Have us both picked up by 'copter.'

'I'll have one on your roof in twenty minutes, sir.'

Damn the lab for taking him so

literally, Ralph thought, as he left the warm comfort of the bed. Not that he could really blame them, his reputation for speed was well-known and it was only human nature that they should take advantage of his own insistence. He looked at his watch and saw that it was not yet four in the morning. Which meant that he'd had barely four hours sleep. Less because Sophia had stolen the hours with her feminine enticement. He looked at her where she lay coiled in sleep and was surprised at a sudden rush of tenderness. Stooping he kissed her cheek. By her continuous use of the words of love, had she come to really believe in the truth of what she said? In arrangements such as theirs autohypnosis was an occupational hazard.

Pausing by the window he stared at the night beyond. It was raining and below the window the city was a carnival of glittering rainbow coloured lights, washes of brilliance reflected from the wet streets, the endless windows, flashing beacons. Behind those lights the majority of the people were asleep, twelve million minds locked in the fantasy of dreams as they sought escape from the pressures of the day and, from them, rose the sickening stench of mental fear.

The terror of poverty, sickness, of having to make a decision, to live with a mistake, of being wrong, of getting sick of having to defend themselves, of pain and theft and emotional loss. A seething cauldron of mental anguish bubbling with the exploding gases of insanity. A bomb nearing the point of detonation.

Frere was already in the annex when Ralph arrived at the neurological laboratory. The inspector lifted a hand in greeting then commented, 'Major, you look as if you've not slept for a week.'

'I'm beginning to think I haven't. Sorry to get you out of bed but you're needed.'

'I don't mind,' said Frere. 'It makes a break from normal routine. And to tell the truth I'm curious. I've never sat in on one of these things before. The only point which puzzles me is why you want me here at all?'

'I told you,' said Ralph. 'You're needed. You know the local area and the local people.'

He crossed to a dispenser and drew a cup of coffee. The shower he'd taken before leaving home had done little to relieve his fatigue and his eyes felt gritty beneath their lids. 'There could be a face you recognise. With luck we could spot the killer and you could name him right away.'

'You think that could happen?'

'It's possible. It's a chance and we have to take it.'

'A thin chance,' said Frere dubiously. 'In my experience the solving of crime isn't that easy. Usually we don't solve it at all. Aside from domestic crimes, that is, we can usually take care of those. And even if we do spot the killer we still wouldn't have admissible evidence. All he would have to do is to arrange an alibi. He probably knows a dozen girls who would be willing to swear that he was with then at the time.'

'True,' admitted Ralph. The inspector, he noted, had apparently given up his previous conviction that the murder had been committed by some irresponsible youngster. 'But if we can get to him fast enough he might not have time to arrange a defence. This technique is still fairly new and we haven't publicly announced it for obvious reasons. So not too many people know about it. The killer certainly didn't. If he had he would have put the bullet through the brain instead of the heart. Incidentally, did you get a report from ballistics yet?'

Frere nodded. 'The slug came from a .38 short barrelled Colt hammer revolver.'

'And the owner?'

'There hasn't been time to make a full check of the records yet. The Central Gun Registry doesn't work twenty-four hours a day as we do. My guess is that there won't be a registered owner. The gun was probably one left lying around after the last amnesty. It's a funny thing about guns,' mused the Inspector. 'Illegal possession can get a man a year in jail and surrendering it can get him a bounty but still they hate to let them go. There must be something about them.'

'There is,' said Ralph. 'Aside from anything else a gun is a power-symbol. An equaliser.'

'Guns are trouble,' said Frere with

emphasis. 'In the wrong hands, that is. A guy gets into a argument, he gets punched in the mouth and he pulls a gun. The result is murder instead of simple mayhem.'

'Perhaps he wouldn't have got punched in the mouth if the man doing the punching had known that he was armed,' suggested Ralph dryly. 'Don't forget, an armed society is a polite one. It has to be.'

'Be polite or be dead,' said Frere. 'I've heard the arguments for and against and I still say that a man with a gun is dangerous. I — ' He broke off as a white-coated technician came through an inner door and gestured towards them. 'Is this for us?'

'That's right.' Ralph finished his coffee and threw the cup into a waste basket. 'Let's go and see what they've found.'

Beyond the inner door were rows of seats, a screen, the humped bulk of a projector towards the rear. A few technicians clustered around it, making final adjustments and conversing in low tones. The man who had called them ushered Ralph and Frere to a couple of seats and handed the major a remote.

238

'This controls the still-camera. If you see a scene you want copied just press the button.'

'Thank you.' Ralph took the device. 'Are you ready to commence?'

'Anytime you say, Major.'

'Then let's get started.'

The screen flared to sudden life and a woman faced them, smiling. She was stunningly beautiful with aureole hair and eyes of an impossible blueness. The face grew larger, filled the screen and was abruptly replaced by a nipple breast. A wide-eyed teddy bear with shining brown fur came next. Then a rocking horse, a ball, a clutter of toys, the barred confines of a wooden pen. Frere sucked in his breath as a monstrous visage followed, seamed, warted, fanged like a pig.

'Sorry about this, Major,' said the technician. 'The probe must have slipped a couple of angstroms but we thought you'd like to see it as we got it instead of the restricted recording.'

The Inspector moved uneasily in the dimness. 'What's happening? Has something gone wrong?'

Ralph spoke in a whisper. 'Just the usual problem. Unless the probe is adjusted exactly right you get a jumble of false-memories. Like the first woman we saw. That was his mother but, of course, she never really looked like that. Olsen has overlaid his early impressions with adult data as to standards of beauty and thought of her as being the epitome of womanhood. One thing it tells us, though, he must have loved her.'

'And the other one?'

'Probably a relative or neighbour whom he didn't like. Hate-emotion colours fact into incredible distortions. What we are doing now is to dig into his mind and recreate his visual memories. Theoretically an entire life could be recreated this way. The trouble is that it would take a lifetime to show. What the technicians do is to speed things up and to skim the surface area. In any case we aren't interested in his early life, only the last few months.'

'The last few seconds would be enough if you only wanted to know who killed him,' said Frere. 'But of course you want more than that. One thing I don't understand. How do you determine the time sequence?'

'That's another problem and the short answer is that we can't. There's no real way of telling to a close degree unless there is external data backing the image. A clock, a calendar on the wall, the date of a newspaper, things like that. A lot of it is a matter of guesswork and intuition. That or an incredible amount of time and patience.'

Ralph settled back in the comfortable chair as the inspector nodded his understanding, The projection room was warm and cosy, the air touched with the scent of pine, the flowing colours on the screen adding to the invitation to sit and relax and yield to mounting fatigue. Irritably he blinked and forced himself to concentrate.

Before him the images flowed in shapes and visions of nightmare, distortions of the reality he knew. Even the stream of faces now appearing seemed, in some way, to belong to creatures other than human. The proportions and colours were wrong as if they were waxen masks that had softened and flowed a little in the sun. Strange, he thought, how one man never sees things exactly as they appear to another. He glanced at Frere. 'Anything?'

The Inspector shook his head. 'Not as yet.'

Ralph looked again at the screen where the memory-images of the dead man glowed in shifting bewilderment. Pictures of exteriors, the interior of a hotel, a shop, the store. Of men and women, most faceless, pale blobs over vague bodies, people met and barely remembered. A succession of flickering blacknesses caused by unconsciousness or sleep. Printed pages, coloured illustrations, a tangle of equipment, the solid bars of a cell and then, abruptly, a face, clear and sharp in full-view.

Frere grunted. 'That one!'

'Hold!' ordered Ralph, speaking to the technician. 'Retreat back to that incident.' He watched as the screen fuzzed and pressed the button as the image reappeared. 'Inspector?'

'That's Sam Bastedo. He looks a little different, but that's who it is.'

'Are you positive?'

'There's no possibility of doubt.' Frere turned, his eyes glinting with wry humour. 'At this very moment he is searching the dead man's store and he's got a friend to help him. We've had the place under surveillance as you ordered and they broke in last night at dusk. From their conversation it's clear what happened. Bastedo had arranged with Olsen to make some dope and now he is trying to find it. We've let them go ahead in order to maintain our security and we might as well let them work for us. They'll be arrested as soon as they leave.'

Ralph was thoughtful. 'Dope? MDM?'

'I don't think so. In any case neither of them killed Olsen. As I see it Olsen promised Bastedo to make some LSD and then found a chance to make something carrying a higher margin of profit. I can let you have a transcript of their conversation, condensed, of course, but you can forget about Bastedo as the killer. He isn't your man.'

'I might talk to him all the same. What will be the charge?'

'Breaking and entering. They've both got records and will probably get three to five years each. They've only been out of Dexter a few days. A pair of amateurs stepping out of their class.'

'I'll take your word for it,' said Ralph and then, to the technician, 'Continue the run. Try and get as up to date as you can.'

'We're on the edge now, Major. We'll waste more time trying to hop than if we just run it straight through.'

'All right,' said Ralph. 'Do it your way.'

Again the flow of images, the endless trivia seen but almost immediately forgotten. Consciously forgotten but never subconsciously for nothing could eradicate the data that entered the computer that Olsen had carried within his skull. Twice Ralph pressed the button as faces came into sharp focus. A third time and then Frere drew in his breath.

'Hold!' Ralph looked at the inspector. 'You know him?'

'No. I thought I did in the side view but now I see him face-on I don't.'

'Try again. Remember there is quite a

bit of distortion. You're not seeing what I'm seeing and Olsen saw different again. Concentrate on the bone structure and the relationship of the nose, ears and mouth.' Ralph pressed the button to register the scene. 'Any luck?'

'Sorry, no.'

Ralph stared at the heavily moustached face and said to the technician. 'How deep is the intensity?'

'It's a long exposure, Major. The image is steady for quite some time. As if they had faced each other for a long period.'

'Or as if they knew each other well and one exposure reinforced the other?'

'Yes.'

'Which is the most probable?'

'It's impossible to say,' confessed the man regretfully. 'There is a third alternative which could be the answer. The image is intense because of a deep emotional significance. There is certainly a deep-register whatever the reason. Shall I continue the run?'

'Yes. Fit a trigger to monitor all repetitions of that particular image.' Ralph looked at the inspector. 'We'll get a succession of stills made and shown through various distorters. Get some artists to work as well. It might be that, with a little alteration, you will recognise who it is.'

'I'll try.' Frere's eyes returned to the screen and the resumed images. 'But he didn't kill Olsen. Not unless he returned to finish the job later.' He grunted as the colours blurred and faded into darkness. 'What now?'

'That's the end, Major,' said the technician as if answering the question. 'That's all we can get.'

'Run the last minute again,' ordered Ralph. 'Repeat until I tell you to stop.'

Hunching forward in the chair he palmed his eyes and then concentrated on the images. The interior of the living room, a door, the interior of the store, a flash of colour and then fading darkness. Frere waiting until it had run through twice and then whispered a question.

'Why can't we see who killed him? The shot came from the front so he must have seen the man. And he had to be close the powder burns prove that. So why can't we see him?'

'We reached him too late, Cellular deterioration had started before the neurological boys could freeze his brain. It's no one's fault but breakdown had already commenced and the most recent memories are always the first to go.'

'So it's a bust,' said Frere. 'A washout.'

'Not quite,' corrected Ralph. 'We've eliminated Bastedo as a murder suspect and, if what you say is right, as a conspirator in the MDM business. Also we've got someone who you still might be able to recognise.'

'A small return for the loss of a night's sleep.'

'True, but who ever said that a policeman's lot was a happy one?'

'Certainly not a cop,' said Frere. He rubbed his heavy features. 'To hell with it. Let's get some breakfast.'

19

They ate in an all-night drug store, the inspector wolfing his food like an animal or like a man so accustomed to snatching his meals that he had lost the habit of leisurely eating. In the bleak light of a wet dawn his face was drawn and aged, the drooping mouth giving him the appearance of holding some private grief, and yet despite his grizzled hair he could not be all that old. Fifty, perhaps? It was hard to tell.

Moved by a sudden impulse Ralph said, 'I'm sorry.'

'For what?'

'For getting you out of bed.'

'Forget it.' Frere mopped up the last of his eggs and stuffed the bread into his mouth. 'I'm used to it,' he said after swallowing. 'I forget just when I had a solid night's rest and I doubt if I could sleep straight through now if I wanted to. There's always something. Kids on the march, a murder, a rape, a stick-up. You name it and we've got it. Being a cop is a full-time job.'

'How long?'

'I started as a rookie twenty-six years ago.' Frere spooned sugar into his coffee and shook his head. 'Funny day. The wife,' he explained. 'She gets a little tired of never having a normal married life. Most of the time I'm at the station. I rarely see the kids and we haven't had a vacation in years. Sometimes she gets a little irritated, you know how it is.'

Ralph sipped his coffee but made no comment.

'She sees others of our age group and gets riled at the difference,' continued Frere. 'If I'd have gone into business I'd be well fixed by now. Hell, the hours I put in I'd have been better off labouring. But there it is. You pick your life and then you're stuck with it.

'Would you do it again?'

Frere shrugged. 'You're in the same business, Major, would you?'

The same business but with a slight difference and the difference was a private income which made him financially independent. A better education too, which had enabled him to join UNLEA and gain rapid promotion. Twelve years, thought Ralph, and in comparison I've had it easy. He knew what it was like to be a rookie, putting up with endless duty for the satisfaction of doing a necessary job and doing it well. But later? When the sullen antagonism of those he was sworn to protect got under his skin? When the world passed him by and he was left with only his uniform, he club, his badge and his gun?

Nobody loved a cop but they were only human. It was inevitable they should lose patience and get a little rough. Knights among the peasants, he thought, remembering Big Harry. There had been truth in what the old man had said.

He rose and fetched more coffee, picking up a couple of newspapers as he passed the stand. Giving one to the inspector he looked at the other.

CANCER NOW CLAIMS ONE IN SIX! read the headline. The legacy of tobacco smoking was coming home to roost. He flipped pages, barely interested in the reports of riots, protests, distur-bances, demonstration. Starvation in Ghana. A drought in India. War in South America. Israel snarling at the Arabs and the Arabs burning Jews. A new message from the Pope calling for universal peace. An outbreak of typhoid in London. He caught an item in the social column.

'Mrs. Cybele Howarth has returned to the city and will be at home to her friends as from this evening.'

Finishing his coffee the inspector rose, folding his paper and slipping it into his pocket.

'I'd better get back to the station. How much do I owe you for the food?'

'Nothing, it's on me.' Ralph spoke quickly in order not to sound patronising. 'I'll let you know when those stills are ready. Better still I'll send them down to the station for you to look at.' Rising he held out his hand. 'Thank you again for your cooperation.'

'That's all right, Major. I only wish I could have been of more help.'

Ralph resumed his seat as the inspector left. The drug store was getting busy as late-night workers dropped in before heading for home and early workers stoked up for the day. Through the window he could see a band of deadheads wandering slowly down the street. As indistinguishable as peas in a pod they searched trash cans for items of value; discarded clothing, books, things they could sell or turn to personal advantage. A street-cleaning vehicle came slowly down the road brushes spinning as it cleared the gutter. Two policemen passed the window, idly swinging their clubs and obviously watching the scavenging youngsters. The tide of life in the city was accelerating towards its daytime peek.

Thelma looked startled as he entered his office. 'Good morning, Major. You're early today.'

He ignored the faint reproof. The secretary had firm ideas as to the propriety of office-hours and clung them despite his casual regard for time. 'Have the stills from the neurological lab arrived yet?'

'They're on your desk, Major, together with the information you requested from the computers.'

'The word-association run-throughs?'

'Yes, Major.'

Ralph felt a small pleasure at Thorne's rapidity. Once again diplomacy had worked better than an outright demand. The man, on his mettle, had shown what his department could do.

Inside his office he slumped at his desk and rested his face in his hands, palming his still-gritty eyes. The breakfast had helped a little and the long walk he had taken afterwards but, in the final essence, nothing could replace sleep. He could, he supposed, call the dispensary nd get some Benzedrine. Certain drugs were permitted to officers on duty but he hated having to depend on them. Their rtificial boost would inevitable be fol-lowed by a worst fatigue accompanied, in case, by acute depression.

Instead he picked up the envelope ntaining the stills from the laboratory, rting out those of the moustached face which Frere had almost recognised and putting them side with an order for focus-distortions and artistic alterations. Once the heavy growth of hair on the upper lip had been removed the inspector might have better luck.

Studying them he noticed a patch of light. It was present in the other photographs and he sat back frowning, trying to remember that it could be. Abruptly he reached for the intercom.

'Thelma?'

'Yes, Major.' Her face on the screen was normal, the embarrassing episode forgotten.

'Call the neurological laboratory and ask them for a still-sequence of Olsen's brain. The last three seconds at ten to the second. I'd appreciate speed.'

He turned to the word-association test results and was studying them when the phone rang. It was operations control.

'Major Mancini?'

'Here.'

'We have received a report from a Doctor Amus Sargil of the Armstrong Building on Apollo Avenue. He claims to have a man in his office who has attempted to bribe him to supply a proscribed drug. The drug is MDM.'

20

The waiting room was all in pink and gold with a rose coloured carpet on the floor and modernistic furniture bright and clean in anodised tubing and sterile plastic. A low table on spindle legs held ashtrays and a scatter of recent magazines and, for those too tense to read, a tank of tropical fish offered a soothing distraction. Ralph looked at the man sitting before it, apparently lost in a watery world of guppies, angel fish, swordtails, black mollies, neon fish and ponderous, slow-moving snails.

Quietly he said, 'Is that the man?'

'Yes.' Sargil was short with a bland face and soft brown eyes. 'I've never seen him before. He just walked in and asked to see me on a matter of urgency. It wasn't convenient but I agreed.'

'How was his attitude?'

'Tense.'

'Would you say that he was an amateur?'

'Very much so and he was obviously desperate. He offered me ten thousand dollars if I would help him.'

'A lot of money,' said Ralph thoughtfully. 'And then?'

'I stalled him and called your bureau. I had no choice under the law but he is a sick man. He needs help.'

'He's selfish.'

'Perhaps, but is that a crime?'

'No.'

'But he knew what he wanted,' insisted Ralph. 'There's no doubt about that? It was MDM?'

'Yes,' said Sargil heavily. 'There's no doubt about that.'

'All right, Doctor. You can leave him to me now.'

Sargil made no effort to obey. 'I think there should be a witness. After all I am involved and — '

Ralph was curt in his interruption. 'If you are innocent you have nothing to fear.'

'If?' Sargil raised his eyebrows. 'You see? Already you imply a doubt. I am guilty until proven innocent. Well, Major, that isn't good enough. My professional standing is involved in this and I have the right to protect it.'

'In that case why call us at all? Why didn't you just throw him out and have done with it?' Because the man could have been an UNLEA agent, thought Ralph, and the doctor knew it. He didn't press the question. Instead he said, mildly, 'I have no objection to a witness. If you wish you can record the entire conversation. I assure you that we do not wish to cause trouble for those who assist us by obeying the law.'

Mollified the doctor hesitated. 'Perhaps not,' he decided. 'It's just that a man in his condition is so easily trapped into saying things that aren't true that — ' He broke off. 'I'm making it worse, aren't I? I'm acting as if I'm guilty by trying to anticipate what may never happen.'

'We all do it,' said Ralph. 'You wouldn't be human if you didn't. But I'm not going to trick him. At least you can be sure of that.'

For logical, not moral, reasons. The man had tried to get MDM from the doctor and would expect to receive it from him, not from someone who pretended to be a supplier and who asked too many questions. In this case it would be best to make a direct attack.

★ ★ ★

Ralph said, 'I am Major Mancini of the United Nations Law Enforcement Agency. You are under arrest for attempted bribery in order to procure a proscribed drug. Please show me your identification.'

The man turned to face him, his dull eyes wakening at the impact of present reality. Slowly he produced his wallet.

'Thank you, Mr. Atwater. Now how about telling me what this is all about?'

'I don't know what you mean.'

'You visited the doctor. Why?'

'I've a pain in my back. Sometimes it damn near kills me. I came for him to look at it. That's all.'

'And did he? Look at it, I mean?'

'Sure. He prodded me around and then told me to wait in here. That's all I know.'

And all your telling, thought Ralph

258

tiredly. It was the classic reaction. No witnesses, no proof, his work against that of the doctor. At least that's what he thought.

Ralph said, 'Is Doctor Sargil your regular medical advisor?'

'No.

'Then why come to him? Why not go to your regular man?'

'Why should I? Is there a law against changing doctors?' Anger was bolstering Atwater's resistance. A false rage born in fear but strong enough for the purpose. 'Listen, I don't have to talk to you. If I'm under arrest take me in and book me. My day will come in court. I'm no peasant to be pushed around.'

Lying, Ralph said quickly, 'Sargil has a recorder in his desk. You wouldn't have known about it but he's met people like you before. He recorded the entire conversation and it had nothing to do with your back. He will also give testimony if he has to. So why not admit it and make things easier for all of us?'

'Why should I? To hell with you. If things were normal I'd — ' Atwater broke off and irritably shook his head. 'Why don't you just leave me alone?'

'If things were normal,' repeated Ralph softly, ignoring the question. 'What do you think this is, a dream?'

Atwater refused to answer and, looking at him, Ralph felt a mounting frustration. It had been the same with Cybele and it was the same with all of them. A stubborn silence. An utter indifference to the demands of law and the obligation to cooperate. A depression and detachment so intense that it bordered on the edge of catatonia. They went through the motions of living as if they were dolls and against that the threats were useless for they wanted only one thing.

Ralph caught the other man by the arm and lifted him to his feet. 'Let's go.'

'To jail?'

'No, to hospital. I want to show you something.'

The ward was a shadowed cavern in which beds ran in closely set tiers over the dull gleam of a plastic floor. An uneasy place filled with sighs and moans and fretful mutterings, the air filled with the accumulated tensions of delirium and nightmare. Slim in her green smock Nanda Devi came towards them her footsteps the delicate patter of birds. Her handshake was firm and cool.

'You have a problem, Major Mancini?'

'Not exactly a problem and it's more his than mine.' Ralph glanced to where Atwater stood close by. 'He tried to bribe a doctor to give him some MDM. I'm hoping that we can straighten him out.'

'An ambiguous statement, Major. Don't you mean that you want him to see things your way?' Her dark eyes held a glint of ironical amusement. 'Never mind. But you should know by this time that you are attempting the impossible. Addiction is not solved so easily.'

Atwater stirred, his voice a rumbling echo in the dimly lit expanse of the ward. 'Addiction? I'm not an addict! What the hell is this all about?'

'I told you,' said Ralph. 'I want to show you something. I suggest that you keep quiet and listen.'

'But I'm not an addict!'

'The concept disturbs you?' The

woman moved to his side and rested one hand lightly on his arm. 'An addict is a person who is a slave to a habit,' she explained quietly. 'And we are all, in one form or another, addicts. But here we are only concerned with those who have formed a harmful addiction to drugs.'

His response surprised them. 'Nicotine, alcohol, tannin, caffeine, acetylsalicylic acid — '

'Tobacco,' she interrupted. 'Intoxication drinks, tea, coffee, aspirin — I could name many more in common, everyday use. And, of course, you are perfectly correct. Those substances are harmful, habit-forming drugs and with unpleasant results. Lung-cancer, dipsomania, heart-conditions, internal bleeding of the stomach — the population would be healthier without them. Healthier,' she repeated. 'But happier? Who can tell?'

Her shoes made small sounds as she led them down the length of the ward. 'Here we have the results of excess. Methyl alcohol, which destroys the optic nerve. Cocaine. Heroin. Morphine. Did you know that many patent medicines if taken in large quantities can produce peculiar side-effects? And so will powdered nutmeg, the smoke inhaled from burning leaves of laurel and the buds of certain cacti which contain mescaline. And, of course, there are always the 'witch plants'; the mandrake root, deadly nightshade which contains belladonna, henbane, the fly-agari mushroom which contains Muscatine, thorn apple, the fresh, underground rhizomes of hemlock, a dozen natural growths which contain hallucinogenic substances. That is why they are called 'witch plants'. The poor women who drank tisanes made from them swore that they'd had actual intercourse with the devil, had flown to covens and done a hundred impossible things. And they had — but only in their own delirium.'

'Dreams,' said Atwater thickly. 'Why are you telling me all this?'

'Because you are an intelligent man and should be able to understand what I am going on about. From the beginning of time men have tried to escape from the world in which they found themselves. All religions are founded on the concept of a better world to come and always men have tried to escape in the region of the mind. And so alcohol, opium, cannabis, mescaline, various types of fungi and distillations from insects and herbs. Chemical to distort reality and to bring euphoria and peace. I am not going to argue the philosophy of their use. For me, as a doctor, they are used and that is enough. I have to treat the end product and, as you can see, it isn't pleasant.'

She gestured to the ward and then led the way to the far end aware partitions had cut off a section of the floor. A continuous strip of one-way glass surrounded it at breast height and a raised step more like a broad platform followed the window. She halted before they reached it.

'One more thing. Remember what I said about addiction. It is a habit and habits can be broken. Unless you want to end up like those you have seen then give it up.'

'Now wait a minute!' Atwater's face was mottled, dark with anger. 'I'm not an addict! I keep telling you that.'

'You've taken MDM,' said Ralph quietly.

'So? What if I have?'

It was an admission, the first, and he was quick to take advantage of it. 'Often?'

'A couple — ' Atwater broke off, conscious of what he was saying. 'You're trying to trick me.'

'I'm trying to help you,' said Ralph patiently. 'I'm offering you immunity if you will agree to cooperate. Who supplied it?'

He had pressed too hard and gone too fast and knew it as he saw Atwater tighten his hands. Smoothly the woman stepped into the breach.

'You don't consider yourself to be addicted, do you?'

'No.'

'It's true that MDM is not physically harmful,' she admitted. 'It does not alter the metabolism as, say, heroin does. That means you will not become physically dependent on it and will suffer no bodily ill-effects if you cease taking it. Nevertheless it is extremely addictive.'

'But — ' Atwater broke off.

'You were saying?'

'All right,' he blurted. 'So I've taken it a couple of times but it's harmless. You've said so yourself. You just take it and dream and — '

'Wake up?' Her face was serious. 'Do you know Shakespeare? Caliban in *The Tempest*?' She began to quote in her soft, musical voice.

"Be not afeard; the isle is full of noises, sounds and sweet airs,
That give delight and hurt not. Some-times a thousand
Twanging instruments will hum about my ears;
And sometimes voice, that, if I then had waked after
Long sleep, will make me sleep again; and then, in dreaming,
The clouds methought would open and show riches
Ready to drop upon me; that, when I wak'd I cried to dream again.'

'That was written about five centuries years ago but it is a literal description of the effects of MDM. And that is why it is so addictive. The user wakes and cries to dream again. Like you. Like those in there!'

She turned and stepped towards the window forcing him, by example, to do likewise.

Beyond the glass the area was totally devoid of any kind of furniture. On the bare floor a score of men rested, most curled in a foetal position, a few sitting with their backs to the wall. All were naked. Many sat in pools of their own urine and excreta.

'The result of using MDM,' she said quietly. 'It is the most potent hallucinogen ever known. It short-circuits the brain so that it feeds on its own sensory apparatus in a closed-cycle feedback system. In layman's language what you think is. Literally. You taste the food you imagine you are eating, the water and wine. You feel the rush of wind and the impact of flesh and because imagination is limitless and you are living in a world of the imagination, there is no restraint as to your activities. Even the time-consciousness is altered so that you live a year in a matter of hours. It is the ultimate in mental-expansion and provides a literal, mental paradise. But using it invariably leads to this.'

Atwater made a choking sound.

'They're in catatonia,' she continued softly. 'So depressed that, if they began to improve, they would kill themselves. That is why we have had to remove their clothing and even their dentures. We cannot stop them swallowing their tongues or ripping off their genitals so as to bleed to death but we do our best. You realise what has happened to them, of course?'

'No!' said Atwater. He was sweating. 'God, no!'

'They believe they are trapped in a nightmare. They have lost touch with reality and think that only the world of MDM is real. That is why they will kill themselves if they think of it as a means to escape from what is, to them, a literal hell.'

Taking advantage of Atwater's shocked condition Ralph said, 'Who supplied you with the drug?'

'A friend.'

'His name?'

'Ned Lacey. But it won't do you any good to chase him.' Atwater lifted a trembling hand and wiped the sweat from his forehead. 'He's dead,' he said dully. 'Someone's killed him.'

21

He lay where he'd fallen, one hand extended as if in supplication, his head a mass of blood and brain and sticky hair. Ralph watched as men lifted him to a stretcher and carried him away reminded of another corpse in another place and wondering why all dead men looked the same. It was the emptiness, he decided, the loss of individuality that made each man unique.

'I saved him for you to look at,' said Frere. His heavy face was grey with fatigue and he looked older than he had earlier that morning. 'The neurological boys said there was no point in saving the head as the brain was too badly mangled to be of use. He died about the same time as Olsen.'

'How close?'

'Maybe an hour either way. This place is air-conditioned and would have retained the heat of the body but call it between forty and forty-three hours ago. The doctor wouldn't be more precise until he's done an autopsy.'

'It's close enough. Did you know the dead man?'

'Lacey was a pimp,' said Frere dispassionately. 'A fixer. No record but a bad reputation. If you wanted something he'd do his best to get it and most times succeed. At a price, of course.' His sombre eyes narrowed with speculation. 'Do you think he could have been working with Olsen?'

'I'm not sure.' Ralph took some photographs from the envelope he carried. 'I've had these altered. I was going to send them to you but decided to bring them instead. Lacey?'

Frere nodded. 'There's no doubt about it. Even with the moustache he looked familiar and without it I'd know him anywhere. So he had been meeting Olsen and in disguise. But why?'

'We know why,' said Ralph. 'Olsen had been making MDM and he needed a distributor. Lacey must have been his outlet. We know that he was handling the stuff.'

He looked around the apartment. It was a small place with cheap furnishings and soiled walls but had once been comfortable enough. Now everything was chaos with clothing, books, papers and drawers scattered over the floors. The bed had been ripped apart and the mattress was a jumble of fabric and springs. Even the contents of the refrigerator had been flung about the kitchen to mingle with the spilled contents of emptied containers.

'It was like this when we arrived,' said Frere. 'Even the corpse had been rifled and robbed. His wallet was empty,' he explained. 'All he had was a few loose coins. If there was any money in this place it isn't here now. I suppose Atwater took it.'

'He wasn't after money,' said Ralph. 'He said that the place was a mess when he arrived but he made it worse looking for what he'd come for. Lacey had been supplying him with MDM and he wanted more. When he couldn't get in touch with his supplier he came looking for him. The door was ajar and he walked in and found the body.'

Frere snorted his incredulity. 'That's what he says.'

'He said it under the influence of pentothal,' said Ralph mildly. 'I offered him immunity for his full cooperation and he accepted. But he didn't kill Lacey. He had the best of reasons for wanting to keep him alive because Lacey was his only source of MDM. That's why he had to attempt bribery and how we managed to pick him up. He'd grown desperate and hoped that his money would talk loud enough to get him what he wanted. A typical panic-reaction, but it happens and, in this case, it ties them together.'

'Coincidence,' said the Inspector. 'What would police work be without it?'

'Almost impossible' admitted Ralph. 'Did anyone hear the shot?'

'If they did they aren't saying.'

'And the bullet?'

'I'm waiting for a report from ballistics. They're going to call me as soon as they've checked it out.' Frere scowled as he looked at the kitchen. 'Damn mess! We can't even make ourselves a cup of coffee.'

'You want that?'

'Sure, and food too. I haven't eaten since we had breakfast.'

'Ask one of the neighbours to oblige,' suggested Ralph. He took more photographs from the envelope. 'And, while you're asking, check to see if anyone in the building remembers having seen this man during the past two days.'

Frere pursed his lips as he took the coloured prints. 'Do you think he killed Lacey?'

'He could have done. He was the last man to have seen Olsen alive and we know there is a connection.' Ralph produced more photographs and spread them on a table. 'These are a sequence from the last three seconds of Olsen's life. A reflection of the light from the door on something bright. Now look at this.' His finger tapped one of the prints. 'No reflection or one not as bright as the others and therefore not as noticeable. Something had occluded the light. I had the lab isolate the patch and blow it up. It shows a man's face. I think he is the man who killed Olsen.'

'Or someone who just looked in at the door?'

'Perhaps, but I don't think so. Olsen must have heard the bell and reached the store as the man was coming in. Perhaps he lingered a moment to make sure the area was clear. It doesn't matter. Olsen died immediately after.'

'But it still isn't proof, major.'

'No,' admitted Ralph. 'It isn't concrete evidence but it helps. The results of the ballistic tests may help even more. Do you know him?'

The inspector frowned as he looked at the photograph. 'I'm not sure,' he said slowly. 'He reminds me of someone but — ' He broke off and headed towards the door. 'Sergeant Kipechne!'

'Here, Inspector!'

Frere handed him the photograph. 'Do you know this man?'

'Why, sure,' said the sergeant after a single glance. 'That's Sutton. The Champ.'

22

Despite its garish opulence the stadium held an animal-smell, the odour of sweat and blood and oil, the miasma of compressed bodies still clinging to the empty seats and seeming to ooze from the walls. In the dim lighting the ring looked a pale square of stained whiteness, an empty alter to violence waiting to receive its next consignment of victims. In the silence the feet of their guide made echoing shuffles a she led them towards the dressing rooms. He was a small man with the wizened face of a monkey and hair growing thickly on arms and chest.

Halting, he said. 'I hope you know what you're doing. The Champ is getting ready to fight tonight. He's not going to appreciate being interrupted.'

'Too bad,' said Frere. 'Where is he?'

'Down there.' The man jerked his head towards a narrow passage. 'Third door on the left.' His voice rose in obvious warning. 'Damn cops! Coming in here and upsetting the routine! If I was the Champ I'd teach you a lesson.'

'All right,' said Frere. 'Now that you've told him we're coming make yourself scarce.' He lowered his voice as he followed Ralph down the passage. 'Watch yourself, major, I don't like the idea of you going in there alone. He could make trouble.'

'We've been through all that,' said Ralph. 'And you know why I must see him alone.' Opening the door he stepped into the cubicle.

Inside the animal-smell was more pronounced as if the very air retained the emotional aftermath of primitive exertion. Sutton was lying on the couch, eyes closed, his face towards the ceiling. Beneath his skin little muscles jumped in irregular pulsations. He was completely nude.

Drawing up a chair Ralph sat beside the head of the couch. Quietly he said, 'I am Major Mancini of the United Nations Law Enforcement Agency. I want to talk to you about a man called Olsen. He owned a little store.'

Sutton gave no sign that he had heard.

He was, Ralph guessed, in a hypnotic condition induced by autosuggestion, the normal preliminary of a fighter readying himself for a contest.

Louder, he said, 'Olsen! Tell me about him!'

Sutton moved a little, his head turning towards the speaker, his eyes opening to show the flash of whiteness against the ebon of his skin. 'You said something?'

'You heard what I said.'

Slowly the fighter raised himself on one elbow. His breathing had accelerated a trifle but otherwise he was perfectly composed. 'You must be joking,' he said without emotion. 'What would I know about this Olsen character?

'We have proof that you were the last person to have seen him alive.'

'Proof?'

'We have a technique by which we can resurrect the images from a dead brain. Your image was among them. The last.' Ralph saw the skin constrict a little, a pulse of tensed muscles immediately relaxed.

Sutton said, 'Is that your way of saying I killed him?'

'Did I say that he had been killed?'

'Would you be taking all this trouble if he'd died of old age?' The fighter swung his long legs over the edge of the couch and sat upright. 'So you found my picture in his mind but what does that prove? He could have seen me fight or I could even have brought something from his store.'

'Did you?'

'How would I know that? I didn't know the man or where his store was. I just said that he could have seen me there.'

Clever, thought Ralph watching the impassive face. Quick and smart and under almost perfect control. But he was at a disadvantage. No one could hide all their subconscious physical reactions when they were naked and in full view.

Casually he said, 'Do you know a man called Lacey? Ned Lacey?'

'No,' said the fighter and added, 'Look, this may not mean anything to you but I have to go into the ring soon. I'd rather not have anything on my mind when I do it. Understand?'

'You won't be going into the ring,' said Ralph. 'Lacey is dead. He was killed by the same gun that shot Olsen. We have proof of that. And you were seen in Lacey's apartment building. We have witnesses who recognised you from a photograph we took from Olsen's brain. I want to know why you killed them.'

'I didn't.'

Quietly Ralph said, 'Why lie about it? I told you that we have proof you did and we can get more. You've heard of drug therapy?'

'Truth drugs?' Sutton looked contemptuous. 'What are you trying to sell me? Do you think I'm that ignorant? You've got no right to use drugs on me and you know it. I know about the law, man! I've had to learn the tricks you people use! You can't frighten me with your big words.'

'Finished?'

'You goddam cops are all the same. You wave the big stick and expect us to cringe. Well, you've got the wrong man this time. I know my rights.'

The anger was genuine, the eyes reddening with aroused fury, a sheen of sweat glistening on the skin. Ralph watched for a moment, impassive, then said, 'I told you that I'm an UNLEA man not a local officer. Now I'll tell you something else. Under the UN Drug Offences Act you have no rights. If you doubt me, ask a lawyer.'

'Drugs?' Sutton looked baffled. 'What's that got to do with it?'

'Olsen was making and Lacey was selling MDM. I think you were working with them.'

'That's crazy!'

'Prove it.'

'But how?' Sutton shook his head and looked down at Ralph. 'Man, I hadn't anything to do with stuff like that.'

'All right,' said Ralph. 'Then why did you kill them?'

'Are you out of your mind? Do you really think I'm going to confess to a double murder?'

Ralph was casual. 'Why not? If you can get something out of it?'

'Such as?'

'I've the power to grant immunity. I'm not really interested in the murders only in the traffic of drugs. If you agree to cooperate it will save us all a lot of time and trouble.' He rose and stared into the fighter's eyes. 'I want to know what has happened to the stuff Lacey was selling. The MDM. Did you find it when you searched his apartment?'

'No, I — ' Sutton broke off conscious of his near-betrayal. 'I don't know what you're talking about.'

'But you did search?' Ralph showed his impatience. 'Come on, Sutton! I haven't got all day. If you want to take advantage of my offer then talk! Did you kill Lacey?'

'You'll give me immunity? You won't prosecute?'

'I give you my word that you won't be charged with either of the murders. Now talk. You killed Lacey?'

Sutton nodded. 'We had an argument. He had a gun and I grabbed it. It went off and killed him.'

'And Olsen?'

'He saw me as I left the apartment. I trailed him back to his store and let him have it.'

'You wanted to eliminate a witness, is that it?'

'Yes.'

'And, after you killed Olsen you went back and searched the apartment?'

'No. I did that before I left. Lacey used to flash money around and I wanted to find it.'

'Just that? You were only looking for money?'

'I swear it!'

'All right,' said Ralph. 'Don't get excited.' He stepped back as the fighter slid from the couch, watching as the man crossed to the shower and held his head beneath the spray. 'When you were searching did you notice anything like a yellow powder? It would have looked something like a mustard and been in a small container of some kind.'

Sutton shook droplets from his hair. 'No. I was just looking for money. If it wasn't cash I wasn't interested.'

'Did you find it?'

'Money?' Sutton shrugged. 'He had some in his wallet and a few hundred dollars hidden in a drawer.'

The fighter had recovered his composure, his face resuming its impassive mask. Ralph said, 'How well did you know Lacey?'

'Not that well. He hung around the fights and wanted to get known.'

'Then why did you go to see him?' Ralph was insistent. 'What was the reason? You said you had an argument, what was it about?'

Sutton hesitated. 'Bets,' he said finally. 'I'd arranged for him to lay some money for me and he didn't want to pay what he owed.'

'So you had an argument, he produced a gun, you struggled with him and it went off and shot him. Right?'

'Yes, it happened just as I said. An accident.'

'And Olsen?'

'I told you about him. I was afraid and had to stop him talking.' Sutton moved towards a locker and produced a robe. 'You promised me immunity,' he reminded. 'You said there would be no charges.'

'Only if you cooperated,' said Ralph. 'I was hoping you could give me the MDM.'

'I haven't got it. Damn it, man, you can

search me if you want! It isn't here and it isn't at home. I wouldn't know it if I saw it. That's the truth!'

'We'll search,' said Ralph. 'We'll turn your place inside out. What did you do with the gun?'

'I threw it into a trash can.'

'We'll find that too and you will help us.' Ralph moved towards the door of the cubicle and opened it. 'All right, Inspector. He's all yours.'

'Now wait a minute!' Sutton balled his fists as he glared at the two men. 'What is this? You promised me immunity!'

'Only as regards the murders of Olsen and Lacey,' said Ralph. 'But there's something else.'

'You bastard! You tricked me you dirty, white — '

'I'm arresting you for the murder of Mrs. Irene Long,' interrupted the Inspector. 'She was found dead in her apartment and the place had been robbed. The gun used to kill Lacey and Olsen was a weapon registered in her name and so we have a record of its ballistic markings.'

'Lacey had the gun! I told you that!'

'Are you saying that he killed the woman?'

'He could have done. I wouldn't know.'

'There's a damn lot you don't know.' Frere was tired and out of patience. 'The woman had been smothered to death and there were bruises on the back of her neck where she'd been held down. The prints will match your hand. And seminal fluid is as individual as a fingerprint. You left enough of it around and it will be simple to check. That's not counting the fingerprints we found on the glass you used and on the handle of the whip.'

'You're lying!' said Sutton. 'I — ' He broke off, face hardening with rage.

'You wiped them off,' said Frere. 'Sure you did, but we've still enough evidence to put you away for life. Get dressed and let's go — Champ!'

'You bastards! You dirty, stinking, white cop bastards! You — '

Sutton made a choking sound as he stepped forward, hands lifting to strike, then froze as he saw the gun in the Inspector's hand, and on his face, the grim determination to shoot.

23

In the elevator Hilda said, 'Ralph, are you sure? I don't know this woman. Have you any right to bring me to her party?'

'It isn't a party. It's just a gathering of her friends.'

'That makes it worse. I can hardly be called a friend.'

'You have to start somewhere,' he said patiently. 'In any case Cybele is always pleased to meet those who are beautiful, intelligent, amusing or interesting. You win on at least three counts.' He smiled down at her anxious face. 'Don't be worried. She won't throw you out and you could meet some useful people.'

'Is that why you invited me?'

'Partly,' he admitted. 'I don't like to see you beating your head against a wall for no return. These people have influence and it wouldn't hurt you to know them. But there's another reason. Cybele badly needs friends. I mean real friends, not the usual bunch of sycophants hanging around. If she takes to you, you could do a lot for her.'

'You make it all sound so very logical, Ralph,' she said as the elevator came to a halt. 'Now remember that I am a woman and tell me the real reason.'

'I wanted your company,' he said. 'Better?'

'Much better.'

Cybele came towards them as they entered the apartment. She wore a loose gown of shimmering silver and looked as cool and as self-possessed as an icicle. Her smile was mechanical.

'Ralph! How good to see you! And your friend?'

'Mrs. Hilda Hickstead,' he said. 'An attorney. She works for Defence.'

'How interesting! You must really tell me all about it later. In the meantime I think you should meet Judge Winton. I'm sure that you have a great deal in common.' She turned, calling and the judge came towards them. He was an old man with a regal mien and gravely shook hands with Hilda as Cybele made the introductions.

'Defence?' he rumbled. 'Ah, yes, a most interesting legal development. But don't you think my dear, that the profession . . . ' The rumble faded as he led her away.

'Thank you,' said Ralph. 'That was kind.'

'Are you in love with her?'

'No, but she is lonely and she needs friends.'

'We all need friends.' She looked at him, her face expressionless. 'Who was it said that the definition of a real friend is someone who will help you to get rid of the body without asking questions?'

'I don't know, but it couldn't have been a lawyer.'

'Nor a policeman?'

'No.'

'Which means, of course, that neither can ever be considered to be true friends.' Her eyes met his for a moment and then she said, lightly, 'You're looking tired, Ralph. Working too hard?'

'Something like that. But you look superb. Travel must agree with you. How was Nigeria?'

'Hot and dirty and fascinating. I brought someone back with me. I'll send him over so you can talk.'

Ralph watched as she moved away, slim and graceful and completely relaxed, in direct contrast to when he had last seen her when she had been as tense as a wound spring and hysterical in her pleading.

'Major Mancini?' The Ibo was tall and impeccably dressed in a conservative suit of charcoal grey. His handshake was firm and cool. 'Ibadan Kaduna, Under-secretary to the Minister of Finance. Our hostess tells me that you work for the United Nations.'

'For the Law Enforcement Agency,' said Ralph.

'A fine, dedicated body of men. It must distress you to see the ravages caused by the indiscriminate misuse of drugs. We too have that problem but nowhere as severe as you have in the West. There is so much to do,' he explained. 'And hard, satisfying work is a great deterrent to those who would abuse their systems.'

'Are you saying that narcotic addiction

is the result of an overabundance of leisure?'

'But, of course! Can there be any doubt? Boredom is the great enemy of the working classes. Unless they are kept active they will grow dissatisfied with their position in life and begin to envy their betters.'

'Is that bad?' asked Ralph. 'To be envious, I mean. Surely it is a help to progress?'

'A help, yes,' admitted Kaduna. 'But once a man recognises the need to improve himself he grows beyond his class. And rightly so. It is the masses who have to be kept beneath firm control for they want without being willing to make personal sacrifices in order to obtain. Work is the best catharsis for such people,' said the Ibo. 'And, in his day he was right. But now we have a new unifying force, the State. In order to combat the enemies around us we must all work for the good of the nation.'

'Three cheers for the enemy!' said Rigby. He had joined them and was obviously a little drunk. The critic nodded to him and Kaduna. 'I see you two know each other. What do you think of his contention, Major?'

'Which one?'

'That they all have to band together against the enemy.' Rigby took a sip from his glass. 'The good, old, faithful enemy. Every government has to have one because it is the big stick with which to beat those who pay the bills into submission. You want a little more freedom? You can't have it because it will help the enemy. You want to cut down on taxes, Impossible! We need the money to protect you from the enemy. Which enemy. Which enemy? That doesn't matter. Anything will do. Popery, Communism, Al-Qaeda, Terrorists, the Chinese, anything at all. And if you run out of external enemies you know what to do? You find an internal one. Use the strength of the people against themselves by putting a villain under every bed. Remember the witch-hunts? A convenient enemy. Drugs? The best one yet.'

Ralph said, 'You're drunk.'

'I've been drinking,' corrected Rigby. 'Once that was against the law because the demon alcohol was made the enemy.

Remember Hitler? He turned a nation against its own people, the Jews. Remember Stalin? He was against the intellectuals.' He swayed towards the Ibo. 'And you. Talking about being surrounded by enemies! For God's sake who in their right mind would want to take over your country? What have you got to offer but trouble? You should take a lesson from the sophisticated West. Find an internal enemy and really bring the big stick to bear. That's the way to have your cake and eat it.'

'You will pardon me, Major,' said Kaduna with quiet dignity. 'I do not find this conversation to my liking. Perhaps we shall have an opportunity to talk later.'

Rigby smiled as he moved away. 'That's one thing about the underdeveloped countries. None of them can stand to be criticised.'

'Maybe he has reason,' said Ralph. 'He's old enough to have been in civil war.'

'We've all been in a war. We're still in it. It goes on all the time and it's called the battle of life. Is that any reason to be so touchy?'

'Perhaps not. Is Dwyer around?'

'Up on the roof, I think.' Rigby emptied his glass. 'You want a drink?'

'Not just yet.'

'Suit yourself, Major.'

The sky had cleared and the night was fine with a glitter of stars framing the glowing tail of the comet. Ralph looked at it and then saw the figure leaning against the parapet, smoking. Dwyer turned as he approached.

'Hello, Major. I see that you've been busy. A triple murder solved all at once. Congratulations.'

'That was a local matter.'

Dwyer shrugged. 'True, but you had a hand in it according to my sources. But why did Sutton kill Lacey?'

'Lacey was a fixer. He'd arranged the rendezvous between the dead woman and the fighter and he guessed that Sutton had killed her. He tried to cash in on his knowledge by getting Sutton to throw a fight. Sutton couldn't do it or he would have run afoul of the Syndicate. He'd stolen the gun and used it to keep Lacey quiet. He had to kill Olsen for the same reason.'

'And the two men who searched Olsen's store?'

'What is your interest in that?'

'Curiosity.' The red coal of his cigarette lit Dwyer's thin, intent features. 'I used to be a journalist and I've maintained my contacts. UNLEA business is regarded as news. Not always available for printing, of course, but still news. What will happen to them?'

'They'll be sent back to prison for breaking and entering.'

'That all?'

'Yes, they didn't find anything.' Casually Ralph added, 'But you would know about it.'

The red tip of the cigarette brightened as Dwyer inhaled smoke.

'Writers are peculiar people,' said Ralph quietly. 'They deal in words and ideas and quite often they believe the things they say. A writer, if he is a good one, will always put a little of himself into everything he produces. And they get into the habit of saying things in a certain way, using phases and analogies and combinations of words that become as individual as a fingerprint. You, for example. You've a reputation for unconventional work and some of your books have a heavy content of propaganda. In most circles you are regarded as a bit of a rebel. A harmless, amusing, at times irrational opponent of the Establishment. Most people don't think you are being serious. I am not one of them.'

'Should I thank you for that, Major?'

'I ran a word-association test between your works and some pamphlets I took from the Society for the Preservation of Individual Liberties. According to the computer you wrote several of them. It would seem that you aren't the harmless rebel most people like to think — and which you are content they should think.'

'The dissemination of information is no crime, Major.'

'Does that include the knowledge of how to manufacture MDM?'

Dwyer smiled. 'Now you're being ridiculous. How the devil would I know that?'

'You are a writer and writers are a privileged class. They can go almost anywhere and ask for all manner of information on the grounds that they are conducting research. It wouldn't be hard for an intelligent man to piece together the formula for the manufacture of MDM. You could even have had help. That doesn't matter. The thing is you did it and I know you did it. I am curious as to why.'

'You know what curiosity did, Major.'

'You knew Olsen,' Ralph continued, ignoring the comment. 'Your picture was in his mind. You supplied him with the formula, which you had either copied with your left hand or had someone copy. You couldn't be sure of it and needed to have it tested and, perhaps, made simpler. When he'd done that he was to have posted it to the SPIL people for distribution. Unfortunately for your plan Sutton killed him before he could do it.' His voice hardened. 'What happened to the stuff he made?'

'Assuming that everything you've said is correct,' said Dwyer calmly, 'and I'm not saying that it is, what makes you think he made any of the stuff at all?'

'He had money and we know that he was supplying Lacey. He'd made it and sold some of it because he was greedy and couldn't resist the temptation of cashing in. But he would have kept his part of the bargain for two reasons. One he wouldn't have dared risk a reprisal and, two, he wouldn't have wanted the stuff found on his premises. Ten years in jail teaches a man to be careful. Olsen was old but he was no fool. He would not have risked spending the rest of his life in Dexter. I think he sent it to the person who had given him the formula and that his supplying it was a part of the bargain.'

'An interesting speculation,' said Dwyer. He lit a fresh cigarette. 'But what has all this to do with me? Do you think I have it?'

'Perhaps at first but no longer. I've seen Cybele.'

'A charming woman, Major. A person who can appreciate a real friend.'

'Is that what you call yourself?'

'It is what she calls me. Unfortunately for you she does not hold you in the same regard, I do not think you will be invited

298

to any more of her parties.'

'I'll survive,' said Ralph curtly. 'But she won't. Not while she has access to MDM.' He thought of the hospital ward and the living vegetables he had seen beyond the partition and fought his rising anger. 'It's in Lagos, of course. Posted out of the country in the guise of medicine. Sent to a convenient address and picked up when she's not there. Simple and safe because the recipient wouldn't know what was in the package and couldn't be touched if it was found. Damn you, Dwyer! Do you hate her so much?'

'Nigeria is a country in the throes of economic development,' said the writer softly. 'Eager to attract those with wealth and so careful not to offend those who have it. Cybele is very fond of Lagos. I've an idea that she will be visiting Africa quite often. In fact she could even take up residence there.'

'Not if we've anything to do with it!'

'UNLEA?' Dwyer shook his head. 'You overestimate your importance. Oh, you're strong enough when it comes to dealing with the have-nots, but if you try telling your bosses what to do you'll find yourself in trouble. And they are your bosses, those with the money and influence and power. The real power. The ability to have you broken if you step one foot out of line. Forget it, Major. There's nothing you can do. Not to her and not to me. There's no proof and you know it.'

'I'll accept that,' said Ralph. 'Because I have to, because I've no choice. But why should you have risked so much? For money? For love of Cybele? What made you do it?'

'For freedom,' said Dwyer simply. 'You said that I was regarded as a rebel, well I am. Have you ever stopped to ask yourself why the government is so against the use of drugs? Never mind that it is against the law, we both know who makes such laws, and don't tell me it is a regard for health and life when automobiles are allowed to kill and maim people by the thousand every day. The real reason is the lust for power. Power, Major, the Establishment is insane with the desire to possess it. What else have they got? Money can only buy so much and a man can only sleep in one bed at a time. The real joy of wealth and position. Slavery, Major. Slavery!'

'We have no slaves.'

'No? What else would you call a man with a load of debt and a job that pays well? What else makes him kiss backsides and eat metaphorical dirt and lose his self-respect of the whip and the carrot? But if a man had all he needed. If he could lift two fingers and tell the Establishment to go and stuff itself, what then? Money would have lost its value and millionaires would have to empty their own garbage. Worst of all they wouldn't be able to give orders and see their hired lackeys jump to obey. And obedience, Major, is the one thing Big Brother can't do without. Because without it he is nothing.

'So if I can spread information I'll do it. If I can help people to be free I'll do that too. But most of all I'll attack the people on the top. The Establishment. Those to whom the rules and laws don't apply because they consider themselves to be a superior race. If they want to poison themselves then let them do it. If they get so jaded they want to escape from their nests of luxury then why should they be stopped? Both ends, Major, from the bottom and from the top. That's the only way we're ever going to smash this cocoon they've wrapped around us. Let the people be free and, if they want to ride to hell in a bucket, let them. What else is freedom all about?'

'You swine!' Ralph was thinking of Cybele. 'You damn Judas!'

Dwyer shrugged and plopped his cigarette over the parapet, watching as it fell. 'You'd like to throw me after it, wouldn't you? But you won't because you're afraid of losing your job, your power, your nice, snug, comfortable life and all the luxuries you didn't have to work for. And killing me would make no difference at all now. The secret's out and there are plenty to spread it around. Soon you'll be able to get MDM anywhere. Freedom in a pinch of dust. So to hell with you, Major Mancini. To hell with you and all those like you!'

Alone Ralph drew a deep breath as he looked at the comet and wondered what the world would be like when it next returned. He heard footsteps and caught the scent of perfume. Turning he saw Hilda, her face a pale oval in the heavenly light.

'Ralph?'

'Over here.'

She joined him and stood very close as she looked at the sky. 'It's so peaceful up here. So very quiet.'

'Like a bomb,' he said, voicing his thoughts. 'One with a short fuse.'

'What?'

'Nothing. Do you like the comet?'

'It's beautiful,' she said. 'Beautiful,' and added, 'Judge Winton, the man I was speaking to, was talking about it. He said that the ancients used to believe that a comet signalled the end of the world. Silly, isn't it?'

THE END

We do hope that you have enjoyed reading this large print book.

Did you know that all of our titles are available for purchase?

We publish a wide range of high quality large print books including:
Romances, Mysteries, Classics
General Fiction
Non Fiction and Westerns

Special interest titles available in large print are:
The Little Oxford Dictionary
Music Book, Song Book
Hymn Book, Service Book

Also available from us courtesy of Oxford University Press:
Young Readers' Dictionary
(large print edition)
Young Readers' Thesaurus
(large print edition)

For further information or a free brochure, please contact us at:
Ulverscroft Large Print Books Ltd.,
The Green, Bradgate Road, Anstey,
Leicester, LE7 7FU, England.
Tel: (00 44) **0116 236 4325**
Fax: (00 44) **0116 234 0205**